MORE THAN THIS

TT KOVE

ARCTIC CIRCLE PRESS

CHAPTER 1

I didn't know what woke me, but I blinked my eyes open with a feeling that something wasn't right.

And it wasn't.

Because this wasn't my bedroom.

This room was completely foreign to me.

I froze as there were movements behind me.

Oh no.

I chanced a quick glance over my shoulder and found a bloke lying next to me, sound asleep. He had his head turned away, but his shoulders and chest were bare.

Slowly, dreading what I'd see, I looked down at myself.

The duvet covered me, but as I lifted it a tiny bit to check, I found I had on nothing at all.

Oh no, no, no.

I sat up oh-so-slowly, praying that the bloke next to me was a heavy sleeper. I clutched the duvet close as I slipped my feet over the edge of the bed and glanced frantically around the floor.

My panties lay next to the bed and I quickly slid them on. My dress a bit further away and I had to let go of the duvet to reach for it. I hadn't worn a bra, since my tits were so small, so I slipped the dress over my head quickly.

I couldn't find my tights, but I wasn't going to worry about them.

My purse was on the floor as well, and I grabbed it as I tip-toed away. The bloke on the bed groaned and flopped over, and my heart nearly stopped. But he slept on.

I inched the door open and light filtered in.

I chanced another glance back at whoever it was, and now the light fell on him, I saw he was familiar. *Very* familiar.

It was Jakob. The most popular lad at school.

Who I thought was good-looking, but who had a girlfriend, so he'd always been off limits. It wasn't like I'd ever been on his radar either. I wasn't one of the cool crowd.

Jakob. And me.

Naked in a bed.

Oh no.

Had I had sex with him willingly?

Had he forced himself on me?

Or had he simply had his way with me while I was too drunk to give consent?

But that was forcing himself on me!

I found my shoes in the hallway, and I stepped into them on wobbly legs, then stumbled out of the flat as quickly as I could.

Once I was out on the street, I stopped to look around. I was downtown, right smack in the middle of it, actually.

It was a bloody long walk home in the middle of the night, in only a dress and heels. I'd forgot my jacket in my hurry to get out—but I regretted it now as I wrapped my arms around myself. I should've searched for my tights too.

My eyes burned as I hurried along the pavement. The town was dark and silent. Or as silent as a town our size could ever be.

Tears brimmed and overflowed, trickling down my cheeks.

My feet hurt in my heels, so I eventually took them off. I let them dangle at my side, hitting against my thigh with each step I took.

I only wore my tiny dress. It was thin, no help at all against the cold breeze. At least it wasn't snowing outside.

I reached the park, where I sank onto a bench. My shoes dropped to the ground with a *thud* as I buried my face in my hands.

You shouldn't cry, Maria, I told myself sternly. *Get up and go home. You can cry when you're safely home and in bed, but not here.*

That pep-talk didn't help.

If anything, it only made me feel worse.

I didn't remember anything. I had no idea how I'd ended up naked in a bed with Jakob—or what we'd done in that bed once we'd been naked.

What the hell have I done?

Did I have sex with him?

I was naked. He was naked. It adds up.

Did he use me?

But it was Jakob. He was known as a good guy. Besides being the most popular guy in school, he was also the kindest. He never talked bad about anyone, he always had a smile and a *hello* for people, even those he didn't know.

That was why I'd had a crush on him for a while now. Because he was so *good*. And handsome, obviously.

But whereas he the epitome of goodness—I'd

heard he even participated in several charities—he dated the school's bitchiest *bitch*.

Oh shit.

He was in a relationship and I'd possibly slept with him—or been sexually assaulted by him—and what the hell would happen now?

I cried harder and wrapped my arms around myself, rocking. It was *freezing*, but I couldn't find the will to get up and get moving.

"Hey. Are you all right?"

I jumped approximately three feet in the air at the gruff voice in front of me.

No one's supposed to be out at four in the morning!

I looked up—and found myself drowning in deep, brown eyes that swirled with emotions I couldn't decipher.

His expression, which had been somewhat worried, turned to surprise. His eyes widened, and I thought I saw a shadow under his left eye. *A bruise, maybe?* But those eyes…

I flicked my gaze back to them.

They drew me in.

Minutes went by while we kept staring at each other.

I sat on the bench, he stood in front of me.

He was the epitome of tall, dark, and mysterious —except his thick, unruly hair was blond. But he was definitely the kind of person people would refer to as a bad boy.

Dirty Converse trainers, loose-fitting, holey jeans, a thick hoodie, and a leather jacket. Not to mention the bruise, because it was there.

And I knew who he was.

We had German together, but I'd never once exchanged words with him.

He was the school's resident bad boy. The one with the explosive temper, the one who got into fights, the one everyone kept a wide berth around.

And now here he was, in front of me, *worried* about *me*.

He cleared his throat, feet shuffling.

That brought me out of my trance.

"Uhh, yeah, I'm—fine." I bowed my head, because I clearly wasn't fine. At least the tears had stopped, but that had only happened because I'd been so shocked that someone was there—and then because of my fascination with him, the realisation of exactly who he was.

He shuffled his feet some more. "You don't look fine."

I sniffled and wiped furiously at my face. My fingers came away black, so I could only guess what state my mascara and eyeliner were in.

"It's nothing. It's silly." Except it wasn't silly. It was so far from silly.

"It's not silly if you're crying about it."

I looked up at him again.

He'd buried his hands in his jeans pockets now and his shoulders were hunched. He looked sort of… nervous.

And he, who was known for being a rude arsehole with authority issues, was being kind to me.

"I think I've been sexually assaulted." It slipped out before I could hold it back.

Why am I telling this to him? a voice screamed inside my head.

His gaze darted up to my face, startled.

"Or, I don't know," I hurried to add. "I don't remember anything. I blacked out." My teeth chattered and I wrapped my arms tighter around myself. "Maybe I had sex with him of my own free will. I don't know."

More shuffling from him. "You don't remember anything at all?"

I shook my head.

The waterworks had started up again and I buried my face in my hands again.

Even more nervous shuffling.

"Can you sit down?" I snapped. "That's driving me mental!"

He froze.

I glanced up, surprised at my vehement reaction.

We stared at each other.

"I'm sorry," I said in a low voice. "You don't have to, obviously, you can just go or whatever—" I motioned vaguely with my hand. "Or stay. I don't mind." I blushed, and it flushed all the way up my neck and my cheeks.

He sat down tentatively next to me. He glanced wryly at me, uncertain, as if he wasn't sure he was allowed to sit there.

I looked back, hoping for honest and friendly, but I was sure my general appearance right then ruined everything I tried to convey with my eyes. My mascara and eyeliner must be smudged and trailed down my cheeks—which meant I must look horrible.

I also couldn't seem to take my eyes off him. Now that he'd sat down, the light from the streetlamp over us fell over him, lighting him up, and he looked *good*.

Why have I never noticed that before?

He averted his gaze, taking in the rest of me. My bare shoulders, my shaking arms, my bare thighs and legs, and feet with no shoes.

My teeth chattered more wildly, to the point he had to hear it. I wanted to curl up into a ball, because I was *so cold*, but my dress was so tight and small it would only expose my underwear, which I did *not* want.

He took his leather jacket off, then wrenched his thick hoodie over his head, leaving him in only a light T-shirt. "Here." He handed me the hoodie.

"You'll freeze." I didn't want to take his clothes from him.

He nudged it at me. "You need it more than I do."

I only stared at it.

"Take it, or I'll force it over your head."

He seemed like he would too, so I took it and quickly pulled it on. It was still warm and it smelled faintly of his cologne. *It's a good smell.*

It blanketed my upper body in warmth and I sighed. My legs were still cold, but there was nothing I could do about that.

"Thanks." I looked at him again. He'd pulled his leather jacket back on and zipped it up. "What happened to your eye?"

His hand shot up to touch the bruise. "Nothing."

"You're really going to give me that? After I told *you* why I was crying?" That was hypocritical of him.

He pressed his lips together, head turning away from me. "My stepfather."

"Oh." *Shit.* "Does that happen often?"

His silence was answer enough.

"Are you on your way home after an after-party?" I asked when the silence stretched on.

"No." He sat up straighter, forearms resting on his thighs. "I can't go home. Last time I checked, after I finished work, the lights were still on."

Oh god.

"That bad?"

He finally looked at me again, face set in a hard expression. "Why are *you* comforting *me*? It's supposed to be the other way around."

"I bounce back quickly." Or it was more like focusing on him gave me something else to think about instead of my current predicament.

His eyebrows lifted. "From possible sexual assault?"

Now it was my turn to look away. "I don't know if that happened."

"Can't you, like, *feel* it? Down there? If something's happened, I mean. If you lost your virginity."

I frowned. "I'm not a virgin."

Now he lifted one eyebrow. "Really?"

I glared. "I'm *not*." Why did he think I was?

"Huh." He shrugged and turned away from me again. "You just strike me as a good girl, is all."

"Good girls have to be virgins?" I couldn't let the subject drop.

He shrugged again, but didn't answer.

"And no, I don't *feel* anything. Except freezing, that is." But I would've felt something if I'd had sex, wouldn't I? Even if I wasn't a virgin… I didn't feel any different. It certainly didn't feel like something had been inside me.

Last year, when I put out for my ex, I always felt it a while after we had sex. Looser, sort of. I didn't quite know how to explain it, but there was definitely a different feeling *down there* after sex as compared to before.

"Maybe you should go to the police," he suggested.

"No." I shook my head. "I just want to go home."

"What if it did happen and there's evidence?"

Evidence… Oh no.

$\mathcal{I}$ stared at him with wide eyes, my brain going through everything I'd seen after I woke up in bed with Jakob. As I searched the floor for my clothes, I'd seen no condoms. Used or otherwise.

What if we had done something and we'd done it *bare*?

"Hey." He'd scooted in closer to me and his hand now clamped down on my shoulder. "Don't start hyperventilating on me, okay?"

"I just want to go home," I whimpered.

"You should go to A&E," he pressed.

"I *can't*. I can't go there and say I might've been raped when I don't know. I can't get him in trouble if I don't know he's done something to me."

"Sure, you can. If you think something happened, you go to A&E. The police can figure out if something criminal happened or not."

"What if I had sex with him of my free will? They can't figure that out in A&E, if it was forced or not. I blacked out. I don't remember."

He clenched his teeth. "If this tosser, whoever he is, raped you, he deserves the trouble he gets."

"And if he didn't?" I stared at him defiantly.

Yes, I was afraid of what had happened. Yes, it freaked me the hell out. But I'd never had a blackout when I was drunk before—and I had no idea how I behaved when I was in such a state.

Maybe I'd thrown myself at him.

Jakob, who was the nicest guy in the whole school... would he really cheat on his girlfriend of his own free will?

"I want to go home," I said again when he didn't answer.

"All right then." He stood and held his hand down to me.

I stared at it as if it was a foreign object. "What?"

"What do you mean, *what*? I'm taking you home. Come on."

He bent down to grab my hand and he pulled me up on my feet.

I stumbled and he grabbed onto me, steadying me. "You okay?"

"Yeah, yeah."

He shuffled his feet again.

"Nervous habit?" I asked as I bent down to pick up my shoes.

He shrugged.

"Aren't you going to wear those?" He eyed my shoes.

"I can't walk properly in them." The ground was freezing cold against my bare skin though, but maybe I could run home. That way I'd keep warm.

I started over the grass—and he followed me.

"Shitty thing about being a girl is you're expected to walk in high heels." I didn't know why I started talking about heels, but I needed to say something. "It looks good. Sexy and all that, for sure, but it's hell on the feet."

I pulled my dress further down. It had ridden up a bit as I sat on the bench, and I wanted to shield as much skin as possible from the cold breeze.

He came up on my side. His hands were buried in his pockets again and his shoulders were hunched against the cold wind.

"Do blokes always enjoy it?" There I went again, running my mouth off with silly topics of conversation. "No matter what the girl feels, do you always think it's good?" My ex hadn't much cared about me —which was why I hadn't put out for him long before I dumped him.

"I don't know. I guess." He shrugged again. He seemed to do that a lot.

"I guess as long as you get to put it in, you're all happy."

"Hey, don't judge all guys alike."

I took a step closer to him. My shoulder brushed his upper arm lightly. "You're not like that?"

He tilted his head back to look skywards. "Why are we even talking about this?"

"We can talk about something else." But what?

We'd crossed the stretch of grass now and were out on the pavement, heading upwards out of the city centre.

But it was more difficult to walk there. The ground was hard, and cold, and small pebbles scattered around that hurt when I stepped on them.

"Hop on," he said.

"What?" I turned my head to him.

"My back." He turned his back to me. "I'll carry you."

"You don't have to do that." But it was *so* tempting.

"I want to. You'll hurt yourself, and you need your feet for your dancing, don't you?"

"How do you know I dance?"

We weren't even in the same programme at school. He took general studies, while I did dance. We had all the regular general studies courses as well, which was why I shared an elective—German—with him. But still.

He only shrugged, so no information to get there.

"Ow!" I'd stepped on another pebble, and I bent down to brush it off the sole of my foot.

"Come on. Let me help you."

I hesitated, but the offer was too good to pass up. I jumped onto his back, wrapped my arms loosely around his neck and settled my knees on either side of his waist.

"Put me down if I'm too heavy, okay?"

"Heavy? You?" He laughed.

I rolled my eyes, but didn't comment. I knew I wasn't tall, that I was thin to the point of being skinny. But I was fit. I ate well, I worked out, I danced every day. I was in good shape.

He slid his arms under my thighs, down to my knees, to keep me secure. His calloused hands against my bare skin felt surprisingly *good*.

Not that it should, especially not *now, tonight*, when I was freaking out about what might or might not have happened at that after-party.

Why did I let Iselin drag me there? I should've just gone home after the bar closed.

I rested my head against the back of his, letting my eyes fall closed as his movements lulled me into a light dose.

Everyone said he was dangerous, but he *wasn't*.

Right now he was *safe*.

If I wasn't so bloody cold, I would've fallen asleep like that, on his back, clinging to him as he brought me home. But I was cold, and it was hard to forget about when the wind teased against my bare skin.

"You have to give me directions," he said. "I don't know where you live."

"Just continue straight ahead."

My whole body trembled, but at least his back was warm against my front. It was the rest of me that was a problem.

"Turn in here," I said after a while, and he did. "I live right down the street."

We came upon my house, all big and white and *dark*. Everyone was asleep by now.

I slid down his back, stumbling a little as my feet made contact with the ground.

"Easy there." He steadied me.

I started making my way up the driveway—and he stayed close behind me until I was safely up the stairs and right in front of the door.

That's when I realised my big mistake.

"Shit."

"What?" He cocked his head curiously.

"I don't have my key. It's in my jacket, and it's—I couldn't find it."

He looked up at the dark windows. "Is anyone home? If you ring the bell long enough, they're bound to wake up, right?"

I swallowed. "My uncle's at work. Maybe Ben's home." I pressed the bell.

Dammit. How could I be so stupid as to not look for my jacket? It had my mobile in it too! And my wallet. It had *everything*.

Shit, shit, shit.

"Why can't this be a weekend when Alex and Leo are around?" I muttered, pressing the doorbell again. "Ben's probably off shagging Tarjei."

He raised his eyebrows at me.

I rolled my eyes. "It's what he does."

"Shag people?"

"Pretty much, yeah."

"He your brother?"

"Cousin." I pressed the bell again, quick, then again and again. "We've got no extra keys, because Thomas gave one to Alex, and he hasn't bothered getting new ones."

He shook his head with a small, rueful smile. "I

have no idea who any of those people are."

"Thomas is my uncle. Alex is my brother's boyfriend. He's off at school. He comes back at weekends, usually together with *his* brother, but of course they're not here *this* weekend."

The steps were cold and I shuffled uncomfortably from foot to foot. "Dammit, Ben!" I held the doorbell in.

"Can you ring someone?"

"I don't have my mobile." I closed my eyes, frustrated beyond relief and slowly freezing to death.

"Here." He held his mobile out to me.

"I don't know anyone's number," I muttered, glaring at the phone. Those days where I could rattle of any number but my own was over. Every single contact was saved on my phone—I never looked at the number itself anymore.

"Maria." He gave me a look I interpreted as *how daft can you be*. It didn't help my plummeting mood. "We live in modern ages. Search them up."

Oh right.

I took his phone from him, went online, and searched up the yellow pages. There I searched for Ben, and when his number came up, I clicked it.

"What?" he answered grumpily on the fifth ring.

"Are you home?" My voice turned an octave too high in my panic. He *had* to be home.

"For fuck's sake."

"Please, Ben, I'm locked out. It's freezing out here." I jumped now, up and down, trying to keep the little warmth I had left in me.

He groaned loudly, clearly not happy.

"Give me a minute. I'll be up."

"Thank you!"

He hung up on me without another word.

I handed the phone back. "Thanks, Roar."

He stared at me. "He's coming to let you in?"

I nodded. "He wasn't happy about it, but he is."

"So you're fine from here?"

"Yeah."

He smiled, then took a step down the stairs. "That's it then."

"But—" He didn't have anywhere to go. "Do you want to come in? Spend the night? If you can't go home…" I trailed off, not sure what I was going to say.

He looked down at the display of his mobile. "He's likely passed out now, so it's safe for me to sneak in."

I didn't want him to go.

The realisation hit me straight in the gut. "What about your hoodie?" I grabbed the front of it.

He smiled ruefully up at me. He was already

down the stairs and in the driveway now. "Hold onto it for me."

With that he walked off.

I stared after his back, at how he huddled in his jacket. I should've insisted he take his hoodie back, so he wouldn't be cold. I was about to be let inside, after all, whereas he had a whole walk back home.

I didn't even know where he lived.

The door unlocked and opened behind me.

"Blimey, Maria." Ben's sleepy face appeared. His hair stuck up in all directions. "What the hell are you doing out so late? And getting yourself locked out?"

"I lost my jacket."

I slipped past him inside.

He eyed me, a bit more awake now. "That's all you're wearing? Who's jumper is that?"

"Someone who took pity on me." I stared down at the baggy hoodie, then hugged my arms close and breathed in the scent of his cologne.

"Go take a hot shower before you sleep. Or you'll end up sick." He brushed past me. "Good night. And don't wake me until noon, please." He waved a sleepy hand, then disappeared down to the basement.

I took the stairs two at a time until I reached the landing upstairs. I took his advice and showered, then dressed in pyjamas—and Roar's hoodie—before I climbed into bed.

Once I'd tucked my duvet properly around me and lay curled up, I allowed myself to think about what had happened earlier in the night. About what I couldn't remember.

Shit.

Maybe Roar was right.

Maybe I should've gone to the police.

But it was too late now. I'd already showered.

CHAPTER 3

I woke Sunday morning to a severe case of anxiety.

What hadn't quite crawled up on me the night before, as I'd still been drunk and freezing and crying, now dawned on me full force.

What happened last night?

What did I do?

What didn't I do?

Was I forced into anything?

Not knowing wreaked havoc with me, and I curled up further in my bed, drawing my duvet tight around me.

Damn it all to hell and back.

How could I have been so careless? I never drank

too much, I never had blackouts, I never had random sex with people I didn't know.

That wasn't *me*.

And yet I'd done it. Or possibly done it, anyway.

Or even worse... I'd been raped.

But no, if I'd been raped, I certainly would've felt that right? Girls who were raped weren't aroused by it, so all the natural lubricant didn't happen during a sexual assault. Thus, it would hurt afterwards.

I didn't hurt. Nothing at all felt different.

I inched a hand under the duvet, slipped it under the hem of my pyjama trousers, and under my panties. Then I tentatively touched myself, feeling for *something*. Something out of place... if it hurt.

But nothing felt out of place, nothing hurt.

So I probably wasn't assaulted. That doesn't mean I had sex, but that I likely had it willingly.

Sex with Jakob. Why had my drunken self ever thought that would be a good idea? His girlfriend was a raging bitch—not to mention one of the more popular girls in school *and* our year's *russ* president.

I did *not* want to get into any drama.

Not to mention, my jacket was still missing, along with my wallet and mobile. I should get up and do something about that, close my payment plan and shit, but I couldn't be arsed.

Even if I was pretty sure I hadn't been raped, the

possibility was still there. And it terrified me, especially as I didn't remember anything.

What had I done?

I'd clearly taken all my clothes of. Had I done it myself? Or had he? If I'd done it myself, had I been the one who'd been forceful towards him? Had *I* sexually assaulted him?

If not, if we'd both been into it… now what?

Jakob was hot, sure, but… I couldn't imagine pursuing anything more with him. I didn't want to have sex with him either—and if I had had sex with him, it surely wouldn't happen again.

There is one last possibility…

That we hadn't had sex at all. But was that plausible when we'd been naked? Or I'd been naked, all I'd seen of him was his bare chest. But I was willing to bet that he'd had nothing on underneath the duvet.

"Dammit!"

I drew the duvet up to cover my face, muffling a frustrated sound in it.

Someone knocked on my door.

"Maria? Are you awake?"

I froze.

It was Iselin.

"Yeah, come in." I pushed myself up into a sitting position, but instantly regretted it as my stomach protested wildly.

Iselin came in, gaze lighting up as she saw me.

"Could you get me a bucket?" I asked, as I felt the bile slowly rise.

Her eyes widened, but she dropped something she'd been holding to the floor, and all but ran out of the room.

She returned with a bucket, and she just managed to thrust it in front of me as the vomit erupted from my throat. I clung to the bucket as I threw up and retched and threw up again.

"Damn, Maria." She stroked my long, blonde hair away from my face, holding it up and out of the way of the bucket and my puke. "How much did you have to drink last night?"

Way too much. But I was too busy retching on an empty stomach to manage to give her an answer.

Once I stopped being sick, I fell back down on the bed. I wrapped my duvet around me again and groaned miserably.

Iselin disappeared with the bucket, then came back with a glass of water she made me sip at.

"I'm never drinking again," I pledged.

"So they all say." She smiled down at me. "So where'd you go last night? You disappeared on me. I figured you went home without telling me. Without your jacket and everything."

I blinked at her, then slowly turned my head to look at what she'd dropped on the floor when she first came in.

It was my jacket.

"You took my jacket with you?"

She nodded. "I couldn't find you, so I figured you went home. I took it with me so you wouldn't lose it."

"Thanks," I muttered, grateful for the fact she'd thought of me. Still, I hadn't gone home, had I? I didn't know what I'd done, besides ended up in bed with Jakob.

"Do you want me to get you some painkillers? Or something to eat? It might help."

Iselin was sweet. She always was. Sweet, kind Iselin, who'd been my best friend for years.

"I don't think I can stomach anything." My stomach roiled by the simple thought. "I'll just stay here. Sleep the day away. Hopefully I feel better tomorrow. If not, I'm so skipping school."

She tilted her head to the side. "I didn't see you drink *that* much. We stayed together for a while, and you only had cider with me."

Yes, that was right. So where I had got hold of stronger stuff? Because surely I'd had to got hold of it, with my blackout and all.

Some flashes ran through my mind, of being

29

handed a glass with something clear in it. Of Jakob smiling. But I had no idea if he'd been the one to give me that glass or not.

"I wish we'd never gone to that after-party."

Iselin raised her eyebrows. "Are you feeling that bad? I admit not much happened there, mostly we just sat around talking and drinking, but it was fun. Meeting new people, I mean."

Now that Nik, my other best friend, had moved away, I spent all my time with Iselin. We were loners, we didn't have a group of friends around us. It was just the two of us.

"I thought you didn't like people," I muttered into my pillow. God, but I felt so miserable!

She shrugged. "I don't know. It was okay. The people at that party were nice. Who knows, maybe some of them will actually talk to me at school tomorrow."

Iselin did general studies. Speaking of which, wasn't she in the same class as Jakob and Roar? Because they were in the same class... weren't they?

Roar...

I couldn't believe I'd shared everything with him. Everything of last night, the fact that I might've been sexually assaulted—or voluntarily had sex.

Our conversation had been so *intimate*. Why the

hell had I shared intimate details about myself with him?

No one ever talked to Roar, he was bad news.

"Weren't you talking to Jakob last night?" she asked then.

I only groaned, as I definitely did *not* want to talk about Jakob.

"I don't think I've ever spoken to him, even if we're in the same class and all." She pursed her lips. "There was this one time we sat together during history, but he didn't say anything at all to me. He's so shy, you know?"

Like most girls, Iselin also found Jakob extremely handsome. If she'd had the chance I had last night, would she have had sex with him?

"I don't know," was all I said. "I don't remember."

Now she frowned. "Damn, you really had a lot to drink, didn't you?"

"Mmhmm."

Way too much.

Never, ever again.

"I'll let you sleep then. And I'll see you at school tomorrow, okay?" She stood and brushed down her jumper. Then she bent to retrieve my jacket and hang it over my desk chair. "It's all in there. Wallet and phone, so don't worry about it."

"Thank you, Is. You're the best." She truly was.

"Feel better, Maria." She smiled warmly. "If you need anything, ring me. If not, I'll see you at school." She lifted her hand in a wave, and I made a floppy-motion back.

She closed the door after her, leaving me all alone in silence.

Now she was gone, everything else came crashing back. Everything from last night. My confusion and panic about what happened with Jakob, and my mortification from everything I'd told Roar.

I wish I could forget all of it.

Then again, I'd only have more things to freak out over.

I did not look forward to school tomorrow. But I had to face it, I had to face *Jakob*. I had to talk to him and figure out what happened last night.

But if something bad did happen, he's not going to admit it, is he?

I groaned loudly and dragged my duvet up over my head. Sleep, that's what I was going to do. Sleep the day away. I could freak out tomorrow, when I'd have good reason for it.

For now I just wanted to forget it all.

CHAPTER 4

I hadn't arrived in the schoolyard the next morning before I knew there were trouble brewing.

Iselin, who'd already arrived at school, came hurrying towards me.

"What's wrong?" I asked after one look at her worried expression.

"There are rumours." She chewed on her bottom lip, anxious. "About you. And Jakob. They're saying —" Her eyes grew so wide they were about to pop out of her head.

I frowned, then turned to look at what had got her attention—only to be slapped right across the face.

I gasped, surprised—then stared at the furious girl standing in front of me.

"You fucking slag," Hedda spat, and she slapped me again.

I was so surprised to be face to face with her I let her—but when she drew her hand back to slap me a third time, I propelled into motion.

I grabbed her hand before it could connect with my face again.

She struggled, expression thunderous. Then she dropped her handbag and tried to hit at me with her other hand.

I tried to stop that too, but it got violent, out of hand.

Hedda screamed something as we fought. She was intent on hurting me, grabbing for my hair, which I'd let hang loose, while I tried my best to fend her off.

I didn't want to fight with her!

"Slag!" she spat again.

She managed to get a hit in—and now I was getting angry. I'd never fought with anyone before, but she wasn't going to let me be.

So I slapped her back, the sound reverberating.

It was her turn to gasp in surprise—and then it got really ugly.

We'd both got hold of each others' hair, and we

pulled, and we used our fists— and then we were pulled apart.

There was chaos around us, people gathered.

Someone had their arms around my waist, pulling me back and away from Hedda. She, in turn, was being held back by Jakob.

"You fucking cunt!" Hedda yelled at me, then turned stormy eyes on Jakob. "And you! You slept with *her*?" Now she tried slapping at him, but he grabbed her hands, holding them tight enough she wasn't able to move.

"Come on, Maria," someone said close to my ear and I was turned away from the scene in front of me and brought over to the other side of the schoolyard.

Once there, the arms around me let me go—and I was spun around to stand face to face with Roar.

"Hey." He stared down at me.

I licked my lips nervously. "Hi."

"Fighting on a Monday morning, huh?" He had a barely there tilt of his lips, like he found what had just happened amusing.

"She started it," I said, then realised just how immature that sounded. "I mean—" I closed my eyes, mortified. "I don't know what I mean."

He chuckled. "I know she started it."

"You saw it all, huh?" *That* was embarrassing. Then again, after our last period of time together and what I'd revealed to him, this was nothing compared to it.

"So it was Jakob?" Now he turned serious. "He's the one from Saturday night?"

I nodded slowly.

How weird was it that the school's nicest guy might've done something really bad to me, whereas the school's bad boy—the one everyone thought was dangerous—was here being kind to me?

And he'd taken care of me Saturday night—or Sunday morning, depending on how I looked at it.

"I should talk to him." I tried to glance around him, but he blocked my line of sight. I couldn't hear Hedda screaming anymore though, so maybe Jakob had brought her inside. "Find out what really happened."

He frowned down at me, as he clearly could tell I absolutely didn't want to talk to Jakob at all. "I can find out for you," he offered.

I blinked. "How?" I asked this suspiciously, because I'd heard lots of stuff about Roar. He was more likely to use his fists than his words.

"A lot more peacefully than how you decided to handle things just now."

I looked down and scuffed the toe of my shoe against the grass. "I should do this myself. I got myself into this mess, so I should try and figure out what exactly *this* mess is in the first place." I pressed my lips together. "Though apparently everyone else knows what it's all about, so…" Maybe that was answer enough.

"Rumours aren't always true."

I lifted my head to stare at him again—and all but drowned in his dark, brown eyes. *Fuck*, but he was handsome, even with the bruise under one eye.

"Are you speaking from experience?"

He shrugged, looked away, then reached out to pluck at my jumper. "You been wearing this since Saturday night?"

I'd forgotten I wore *his* hoodie, and I blushed. "Maybe." I stared down at it. I hadn't bothered with a jacket today, only put on warmer clothes underneath. "You can have it back if you want."

The bell rang.

He took a step away from me. "You hold onto it for me."

That's what he said that night.

He smiled then, flashing white teeth—and if I'd been one of those girls, I would've melted at his feet right there.

"See you around, Maria. And if you need my help… I'll be there."

He walked off, and I stood back staring after him like some other idiot.

"Maria!" Iselin came running up to me, grabbing my hand. "Are you okay?"

I turned to her, slightly dazed. "Yeah."

She inspected my face. "I don't think she left any marks on you. It's not like a slap leaves a bruise." Her eyes cut sideways, towards the front doors. "Fists leave bruises."

She was obviously referring to Roar. But I didn't want to tell her about him. Not yet, anyway.

"Why was Roar coming to your rescue?" Iselin hadn't got that part, it seemed.

"I don't know."

She stared from the door to me. "Why did he speak to you? Roar doesn't speak to *anyone*."

I shrugged, unwilling to share any information yet. Roar was handsome, intriguing, and I still wore his hooded jumper.

"We should go in. Classes have started." The schoolyard was abandoned now.

Iselin blinked. "Did you sleep with *Jakob*?"

I shrugged again. "I'm not sure."

I could tell she put the pieces together. "Saturday night? You didn't go home. You had *sex with Jakob*!"

"Shh!" I glanced around, even though I'd already seen we were the only ones out and about. "I don't know, Iselin. Please."

"How can you not know?" Her incredulous expression changed to one of confusion.

"I blacked out. I don't remember anything." But some people obviously knew something, or else there wouldn't have been rumours. And Hedda wouldn't have attacked me. "I have no idea what happened Saturday night. So you can't talk about it to anyone. I need to figure it out myself first." I had to talk to Jakob.

She nodded quickly.

"Who's been talking about me, anyway?" She'd hurried up to me, after all, before school had even started.

"Hedda's friends." She drew her lower lip in-between her teeth. "Jasmin talked about it when I walked by to my locker, how she'd seen the two of you snogging."

"Oh God." I couldn't remember so much as being in Jakob's presence at the party, much less *snog* him.

"I never thought Hedda would actually attack you though." Iselin moved uncomfortably, almost like Roar did. "Are you sure you're all right?"

"Yeah." It wasn't Hedda's violent behaviour I was worried about; if I had slept with her boyfriend, she was entitled to it. Though shouldn't she be angry with her boyfriend instead of me? He was the one who'd done something wrong.

Jakob, who never did anything wrong.

It didn't make sense that he would've forced me into anything.

Then again, drunk people didn't always behave rationally. Though he was the nicest guy alive when he was sober, maybe he wasn't when he was under the influence of alcohol.

"Oh God." I pressed my hands to my face. "I can't believe it. Jakob, of all people."

"There's nothing wrong with Jakob," Iselin said quickly. "Now if it'd been Roar you snogged, I would've been worried."

I froze, then slowly let my hands fall back down to my side.

"He has a psycho girlfriend. That's enough for me." But I reeled from her comment about Roar, because I had nothing to worry about from him. He'd helped me, he'd worried about me, and now he'd pulled me away from a fight that could've got even uglier.

Roar was *good*.

But I couldn't tell Iselin that, not without telling her everything. And I wasn't ready for that, because I wanted to keep it to myself a little longer.

I wanted Roar to myself.

Now *that* left me reeling.

After my ex from last year, and the small crush I'd

had on Jakob for ages, I hadn't been interested in anyone at all. But Roar... he was intriguing, he was handsome, caring.

I didn't understand his bad reputation.

I also didn't hold it against him, because all he'd done was be kind to me. He didn't have to, he could've walked away, but he'd come over to talk to me. He'd given me his hoodie. He'd carried me home —even going so far as to make sure I got right up to my door.

He's a good guy. A great guy even.

And I didn't want to stand there and listen to Iselin talk negatively about him. "I'm going to class."

"Yeah." She hesitated a little before she followed. "See you at lunch?"

"Yeah." I waved at her, then headed towards my first class.

The teacher wouldn't be happy I was so late, but that was the least of my worries.

CHAPTER 5

I stared down at Jakob's Facebook profile, my thumb hovering over the *add as friend* button. I couldn't send him a message without being his friend—and I *needed* to send a message to him.

I couldn't approach him in school, because he was always around other people. Either mates of his, or a miserable-looking Hedda. If she hadn't hit me earlier, I might've felt sorry for her.

As it was, I couldn't care less about her feelings.

I stared down at my mobile again.

Press that damn button.

But my thumb wouldn't *move*. I couldn't press it, I didn't dare, because if I did there was no way back. I'd have to talk to him, had to ask him, and if I got the wrong answer… what would I do then?

"Hey."

I startled as someone sprawled into the chair next to me.

Upon glancing over, afraid I'd have to face Jakob already now—since it had been a male voice—I blinked upon seeing Roar give me a wry grin.

"You figured it out yet?"

I shook my head mutely.

He crossed his arms over his chest as he regarded me with an inscrutable expression.

I chanced a quick glance around the cafeteria— and found several people shooting us curious glances.

It's not so weird, considering Roar's reputation for being a loner and troublemaker.

I didn't think I had a reputation. I kept to myself. I didn't stand out. Except now I did, because the whole school had probably heard by now that I'd had sex with Jakob.

"Are you going to friend the guy who might have possibly assaulted you?" He stared knowingly down at my phone, where my thumb still hovered over the *add as friend* button.

"I have to talk to him. I thought I'd send him a message and ask, but I have to be friends with him to send him a message." Why would his Facebook profile be so private? Couldn't he have it partially open like everyone else, so people who weren't your friend could at least send you a bloody message?

"It's easy to lie over a message," he pointed out drily.

"I know." I pressed the damn button. "I'm just sending him a message to ask if we can talk. I want to meet him for that, look at his face, see how he reacts."

He nodded. "That's good. It's harder to lie to someone's face."

I cast a wry glance at him. "Do you know Jakob?"

"No." He stared back at me. "Does it look like I've got any friends around here?"

"Not a single one?" I had Iselin at least, and before that I'd had Nik too. Not to mention my cousin and my brother and my sister, though we hadn't actually gone to the same school since primary education.

He shook his head.

"What do you do every day then?"

"I go to school, I avoid going home, I go to work, and then I sneak in during the night." He looked away as he admitted it, like he either was ashamed or embarrassed to admit it.

He didn't have any more bruises—at least not on his face. But his stepfather was clearly not a good man.

"Where do you work?" I decided to go with that

topic instead of bringing his stepfather up. We were in the school cafeteria after all—people could listen in on us.

"The gas station downtown."

There was only one, then, the one closest to Burger King.

I glanced down at my phone. It still said *pending friend request*, so Jakob had neither accepted nor declined it. I reckoned that was good.

If he declined, well... that was my answer, wasn't it?

And if he accepted, then I'd simply have to ask for a chat.

"My offer still stands, you know."

"Offer?" I asked, distracted as I continued to stare down at my phone.

"I can find out what happened for you—and get a truthful answer."

"How would you do it?" I locked my screen and put the mobile screen-down on the table.

"I'd ask nicely." He grinned wryly. "And if that doesn't work, well... I reckon pretty-boy wouldn't want his face introduced to my fist."

"Violence isn't going to solve anything." I didn't want him to hit Jakob.

"Isn't it?" He stared at me again, serious now. "If he *raped* you," he said this in a very low voice so no one but us could hear it, "you wouldn't want him to pay?"

I swallowed audibly. "But I don't know if he did."

"I can find out."

"*I* should be the one to find out." I clenched my hands into fists. "I'm not a coward. I can stand up for myself. This is *my* problem." I might be the quiet girl, the one who kept to herself and preferred books over being sociable—but I also wasn't afraid of speaking up if I believed in something, if something was wrong.

I *wasn't* a coward.

So why couldn't I simply walk up to Jakob and face him?

"It's not about being a coward." His eyes moved from side to side as he looked into both of mine. "You're scared. That's totally understandable. You *can* let someone else do the dirty work for you."

It flattering that he offered. "Why would you want to?"

He bowed his head and ran a hand through his hair, ruffling it. "Because."

"That's not an answer," I pointed out.

We sat in loaded silence, me waiting for him to give me a proper one, and him… well, either he was stubbornly staying silent or he was thinking. I couldn't make out which.

"Hi, Maria."

Iselin hovered next to the table, at the other side to Roar. She shot him quick, curious glances, but otherwise didn't acknowledge him.

"Oh, hey." I shouldn't feel disappointed that my best friend showed up to spend our lunch break together, but I *did*.

Roar pushed away from the table and stood. Then he stared down at me. "The offer still stands."

Then he walked off.

Iselin slid into the chair across from me, depositing her rucksack on the chair next to her.

"Why were you talking to Roar?" she asked, confused. "What offer?"

"It's nothing." I sighed. "Absolutely nothing."

She didn't believe me, I could tell, but Iselin was a good friend. She let it drop.

"Have you spoken to Jakob?"

I shook my head, then quickly checked my mobile. No new notifications. Well then…

"Hedda and him were fighting at recess earlier." Iselin took her lunch out of her rucksack. "I didn't hear much, but it definitely wasn't good."

Maybe I was a *home wrecker*. Now that would've been something.

"Maybe they'll break up."

"So what if they do?" I hadn't brought any lunch.

I still felt queasy, but not enough to be sick again like I'd been the day before.

"Maybe you and Jakob—"

"No way," I interrupted before she could even finish the sentence. "Jakob is *not* my type."

"He was on Saturday."

"Yeah, I don't—What was I *thinking*?" That was the million-dollar question, wasn't it? "I'm not that girl."

"What girl?" Iselin propped a spoonful of salad into her mouth.

"The girl who sleeps around. The girl who gets so pissed she blacks out. The girl who has sex with people she doesn't know." I dropped my head in my hands. "That's not me."

"I know," Iselin agreed. "It's weird. That you did all that, I mean. Sleep with Jakob, drink so much…"

"Who gave me drinks? I can't remember *anything*." Someone must've supplied me with them, I hadn't brought any on my own except the ciders Iselin and I had shared.

Iselin's face scrunched up as she thought. "I don't know. We only drank the cider. I didn't see you drink anything else. I don't think I saw you much after, to be honest. Suddenly you were just gone and I couldn't find you."

"We never should've gone there." I folded my

arms on the table and dropped my head atop them. "It's only led to trouble."

Iselin drew in a sharp breath. "Maria…"

"What?" I didn't bother lifting my head.

"If you had sex with Jakob… you used condoms, right?"

I didn't answer, because I had no answer to that.

"Shit, Maria… You're not on the pill, are you?"

"No." Oh God no, not anything else to worry about! "Shit. *Shit!* I have to talk to him. I've *got* to."

One possibility was we hadn't done anything. Just fallen asleep naked. It wasn't exactly likely, was it?

Another alternative was I'd willingly had sex with him. With or without a condom, who even knew. That could lead to pregnancies or STDs, both of which I did *not* want any part of.

Third possibility was sexual assault. That he'd forced himself on me while I'd been too far gone to protest. But I couldn't see Jakob doing that.

Maybe I'd sexually assaulted him?

"Fuck my life," I muttered before thumping my forehead against the tabletop.

"We'll figure it out. Or you will." Iselin reached over to pat my shoulder. "Talk to him. Jakob's nice. He's definitely not the worst person to be in this dilemma with."

"Yeah…" I had to talk to him. But I couldn't approach him at school, and he hadn't answered my friend request.

Nothing could happen until he did that, because I refused to approach him when he was surrounded by his friends—or worse: when he was with that psycho girlfriend of his.

CHAPTER 6

"*A*re you okay, Maria?"

I startled so much by my uncle's question my fork clattered against my plate.

"Oh, yeah, fine." Except I wasn't. I was a nervous wreck

I had no appetite, I only kept moving the food around on my plate. Ben, too, seemed to share that sentiment, though I couldn't begin to understand why he was in a mood.

Thomas didn't seem to believe me, but he never pried. He was okay that way. He let us figure things out on our own—let us come to him if we needed something.

My phone vibrated where it lay screen-down on the table and I grabbed it.

He accepted my friend request!

Now all I had to do was type out a message to him.

Only I didn't know where to even *begin*.

"I'm not hungry." I pushed away from the table and went to dump the contents of my plate in the rubbish. Then I rinsed it and put it in the dishwasher.

Once safely up in my room, I sat cross-legged on my bed with my mobile clutched in my hands.

I'd pressed in on *send a message*, but had no idea what to write.

Hi Jakob, thanks for —

No, that was too stupid.

Hi, I was wondering if we could meet —

No, that was stupid too. Maybe he'd think I was interested in him, which I was decidedly *not*.

I tried several other messages, but deleted all of them. I was usually good with words, especially written words, but not now. I'd never been so nervous before, so much had never been on the line before.

Take a deep breath. Gather yourself. And just send off a text. What was the worst that could happen, right?

Hi Jakob. I was wondering if we could meet up somewhere to talk about Saturday?

Should I mention something about my blackout?

No, maybe keep that to myself for now. If he thought I remembered everything, he'd be less likely to lie. If I flat out told him I didn't remember, he was never going to admit to anything that would look bad on him.

So I clicked *send*.

Now it was all a waiting game.

And he sure made me wait.

I tried to do homework, I had a Norwegian essay I needed to write, but I couldn't concentrate on it. So I tried to do some of the reading required for history and English, but I couldn't focus on that either.

Eventually I put on some music and dosed off on my bed.

It was hours later when my mobile pinged.

I sat up straight, startled and nervous and anxious.

My hand shook as I retrieved my mobile and turned it over, clicking into the Messenger app to see the answer Jakob had given me.

Jakob: Hi Maria. Yeah, sure. When and where?

Me: How about now? Or soon? BK maybe?

Jakob: I can be there in 20.

55

Me: OK. See you.

So that was that. He was willing to meet me, willing to talk. Now I only had to face him. Considering I didn't know anything, it was harder than I thought.

He might be some guy I'd snogged, fooled around with. He might be some guy I'd willingly had sex with—or he might be some guy who'd taken advantage of me, or I'd taken advantage of him.

That I couldn't remember anything drove me *mental*.

I had to get a move on though if I didn't want to be late, so I headed into the bathroom to brush my hair and teeth. Since I'd been sleeping for three hours, I had to freshen up a little bit.

My clothes stayed the same—jeans and Roar's hoodie—but I threw on a thick winter jacket once I headed downstairs. Since it was late, it was even colder outside.

"I'm heading out for a bit!" I called out, not sure if anyone was even around.

"Okay!" Thomas called back from the living room.

So off I went.

It felt a little like I imagined how it would be to

walk to your own execution. I'd have answers soon, and I had no idea what they would be.

Jakob stood outside Burger King when I got there, hands buried in his pockets and huddling in his jacket. He seemed almost scared when he spotted me, which in turn made me scared of what I'd get to learn.

"Hey." He stepped up to me, and he tried for a smile, but it fell flat because his expression was all anxious.

"Hi." I managed a small, wobbly one before I turned to the door.

He held it open for me and I slipped past him inside.

"Are you hungry?"

I shook my head. "I'll just get a milkshake."

He got a Cola—and he paid for my milkshake too, even if I tried to protest.

Once we had our cups, we found the most secluded table—and I was relieved when I saw we were alone in that section, that no one was close enough to eavesdrop.

We sat down opposite each other.

It was hot in there, so I shrugged out of my jacket.

He did too. He looked handsome in his loose jeans and form-fitting jumper. His hair was ruffled in a styled kind of way and he was entirely clean-shaven. Handsome, popular Jakob who didn't seem to handle his popularity all that well because he was all shy and awkward.

I couldn't see him hurting me.

"What is it about Saturday night you want to talk about?" He toyed with his straw, not looking at me.

"Umm." How to even begin?

"*Please* don't tell anyone," he said all of a sudden, startling both me and himself, it seemed.

I frowned. "Don't tell anyone what?"

He blinked, eyes wide and afraid. "No one can know, Maria. *Please*."

No one could know *what*?

I tightened my grip around my cardboard cup, still not sure how to phrase myself so I'd get the answer I needed without having to reveal I didn't remember *anything*.

"I know I messed up." His face flamed red. "I shouldn't have done it. But— I just want to be *normal*."

My frown deepened. We definitely weren't on the same page, here, that much I understood. At first I'd thought he actually had sexually assaulted me, and that he was pleading with me not to tell anyone about it, but... sexually assaulting someone didn't make him normal, did it?

"I've never been able to... with Hedda." He

muttered down to his cup. "I thought… well, I was drunk. And you were there. And we kissed. But I still couldn't do it."

I sat back, lips parting slightly in surprise. "So we didn't have sex?"

He met my gaze, startled. "No." He glanced away, then bad at me again, his eyes widening. "You —you thought we did?"

I shrugged. "I blacked out. I don't remember anything."

He seemed so afraid, so anxious, that I couldn't help but believe him. We hadn't had sex, willing or otherwise. Because he couldn't do it. Not with me, and not with Hedda.

There was only one reason I could think about why that was.

"Jakob, are you gay?"

CHAPTER 7

*H*e froze and stared down at his hands as if they held all the answers. "You can't tell anyone, *please*," he whispered.

Now I felt *sorry* for him.

"It's nothing to be embarrassed about. You don't have to be ashamed." I took a sip of my milkshake. "It's perfectly natural."

He shook his head. "My parents won't like it. And I don't think my friends would either."

"Then they're not really your friends."

He clutched his cup so hard the cardboard was bending in on itself. I wondered how long it would be before his Cola spilled over the edge. "They are the only friends I have."

"You can find new ones. People who aren't judge-mental arseholes."

He snorted, unbelieving. "I don't know anyone who's—" he swallowed, searching for words, "like *me*."

"A lot of people are." I bent forward a little, finally feeling in control of the situation. *I've got this!* "My family are very open and accepting. My brother has a boyfriend. Two of my cousins are gay. One of my best friends is gay."

I felt brave talking about this, and I reached over to grip his hands. "Ben was in the closet once, but he thrived once he came out. Nik could never be in a closet, because he's too obvious for that. And Andreas, my brother, he never really came out, but when he brought Alex home it was kind of obvious."

If I'd known Jakob struggled with his sexuality, I would've tried to get to know him beforehand. Tried talking to him, anyway. No one should have to struggle like he did, about who they were, about who they liked. No one should have to pretend they were something they weren't.

"You're lucky then, to have such an open family." He bowed his head, stared down at my hands covering his. "My parents won't like it. They have expectations."

"Screw their expectations. It's your life. You have

to live it the way you want, or you won't ever be happy." I squeezed his hands. "And you deserve to be happy, Jakob. Everyone does."

He drew in a shaky breath. "Hedda and I broke up today."

"Oh." I wasn't about to tell him my opinion on *that*. I was pretty sure he'd do much better without her. I didn't know her, but from what I'd seen and from what I'd heard, she wasn't the easiest person to be around. "Did you tell her why?"

He shook his head. "She thinks it's because you and I slept together. I don't know who started that rumour, who saw us at that party and started blabbing about it." He met my gaze briefly. "I swear, Maria, it wasn't me. I don't know who did it."

"It's okay." Not that I wouldn't like to know who had been spreading rumours, but it wasn't like anything could be done about them. They were out there—nothing could take them back.

"She kind of hates you," he murmured.

I let out a short laugh. "Yeah, I reckoned. But it's not like I see much of her. We're in vastly different circles, Hedda and I."

"I just feel like I made of mess of your life."

"Trust me, I can handle myself." I finally pulled my hands back and sat down, sipping my milkshake again. "I might like to keep to myself, but I can handle myself if it comes down to it."

He smiled wryly. "Yeah, I saw that earlier today."

I hoped Hedda didn't have anymore plans to attack me.

"You should tell her the truth, though."

"I can't do that." He squeezed his cup so hard again it dented. "I don't know."

I bit down on my lower lip. "Are you parents… abusive?" Was that why he seemed to be so afraid of them?

"No." But he wouldn't meet my eyes.

"Jakob—"

"They've got *expectations*." Some Cola ran over the edge of his dented cup, trickling down over his fingers. "They expect perfect grades so I can get into the best university. They expect me to choose a prestigious career, so I don't have to worry about money. They expect me to settle down with a nice girl and give them grandkids." It all seemed to make him so miserable.

"If you ask me, that sounds extremely selfish."

"What?" He blinked at me.

"They expect this and expect that, but have they ever asked you what you wanted?" When he mutely shook his head, I leaned forward again. "What do *you* want, Jakob?"

"I don't know." His gaze flickered uncertainly. "I don't *know*."

I felt more and more sorry for him. "That they expect you to give them grandchildren… that's so—" I didn't even have words for how selfish that was! "They can't expect anything like that, because it's your life, it's your body. What if you're not made out to be a father? It's selfish to bring kids into this world who aren't wanted, that's what.

Getting kids for the sole purpose of making someone grandparents is ludicrous. If someone wants to have children, then go for it, but never have children simply because it is *expected*. Children should grow up with parents who love them. Parents who won't ever leave them."

He stared at me intently now. "Are you speaking from experience?"

I took a deep breath, trying to calm myself down. "We were wanted, my brother, and sister, and I. We were. It's just that—" I didn't like to talk about this. "My mum died, and it was like my dad died with her. She was his everything. As soon as she was gone, we didn't really matter anymore, you know?" I hated thinking about that time. "And then he hung himself in our garage. Because he couldn't live without her. But he had *us*. Three children—none of us of age—

who needed their *dad*. But he left us, without a single thought to any of us."

Jakob bowed his head again, finger tracing the rim of his cup. "I've thought about it." When I cocked my head in confusion, he clarified, "Suicide."

Something cold slithered down my spine. "Jakob, no. Suicide's not the answer." Maybe suicide was the answer to those who did it—I could understand not wanting to live anymore, but for everyone who were left… "Or maybe I'm being selfish now." I ran my hands over my face.

I'd just told him how selfish his parents were for expecting everything of him. If someone really wanted to die, if they didn't see any reason to live anymore, was it really a selfish act?

Maybe it was the answer for those who did it. They'd be at peace.

"I've just thought about it. Never done anything."

"Do you want to do something?" I hadn't seen my dad in the garage. It was Christina, my older sister, who'd found him. Still, I could clearly remember being picked up from class that day and taken into the headmaster's office. A normal day… until I found out my dad had taken his own life.

I was angry with him, of course I was. I'd been fourteen years old when he died. I'd been angry and bitter and resentful. He'd left us orphaned. We hadn't had a mum in years, and then suddenly we hadn't had a dad either.

I'd never wanted to be as dependant on someone that I couldn't figure out how to live on if they left me. I would never be that person. I wouldn't be my dad.

"Sometime."

Jakob's low voice brought me out of my thoughts.

"I think about it sometimes. But I never do anything. I'm too scared for that."

"What're you scared of?" I couldn't take my eyes off of him. If I hadn't been sitting here having this conversation with him, I never would've guessed he struggled with everything he did.

"Of doing it wrong."

I blinked. I'd expected him to say he'd be scared of the pain, or dying in general. Not that he was afraid to botch it up.

"Jakob…"

"You can't tell anyone, Maria. Not this, and not about me being— you know."

God, he can't even say the word. "Gay, Jakob. *Gay.* It's a simple enough word, nothing at all wrong with it."

He squeezed his eyes shut.

"Why don't you think about what *you* want to do with your life? Not what your parents expect, but what *you* want to do? When you figure it out, you can tell me."

I came from such an open and loving family. That anyone was gay or bisexual or in love with our own cousin wasn't a problem for any of us. That he struggled so much tugged at my heart.

Now I knew nothing had happened between us, I didn't have to obsess over that anymore. I could focus all my attention on Jakob and his issues. That he'd even told me was a huge thing, considering he didn't know me well enough to know I'd actually keep my word.

He seemed sad, and lost.

"I'm sure your parents only want what's best for you," I said, slowly, thinking about my choice of words. "Most parents want their children to be successful. But if you tell them what *you* want, maybe they'll understand? If they don't... well, my brother's boyfriend broke with his parents. We're his family now, he has no contact with them anymore."

Now he seemed startled. "I don't want to never see my parents again."

"Of course not. I'm just saying... You've got a choice. That's all. You don't have to go to that extreme, obviously, but you *can*. If they make you miserable..." And he was miserable. "You should do what makes you happy, Jakob."

He started to squeeze his cup again, but then brought it to his lips to take a large gulp of Cola instead.

"And it's good that you broke up with Hedda." And not just because she'd hit me. "Pretending to be something you're not... you're not going to be happy that way. And it's not fair to her either to be with someone who isn't actually into her."

He nodded slowly. "You're okay, Maria." He gave me a small smile before he bowed his head again.

"So are you." What everyone said about Jakob was true; he was a very kind person, and shy. But no one had ever mentioned him being so insecure, and closeted, and miserable. So he'd kept many of his cards clutched tight. So tight no one had been able to see it.

Until me—right here and now.

I wasn't sure I was worth that trust, considering I'd half-dreaded he'd sexually assaulted me while I'd been too drunk to give consent. But of course he hadn't done it, he was a nice guy. I didn't think he would've done something like that if he'd been straight either.

"I'll keep your secrets, Jakob," I said. "And if you ever need to talk, I'm here. Also, if you want to meet some gay guys, I can introduce you to some. My cousin Ben might try to shag you if he's in the right mood, but otherwise he's great."

Jakob spluttered adorably.

"I'm kidding." I held my hands up in the universal sign of peace. I wasn't exactly though, Ben *was* a slag. But considering the mood he'd been in lately, I didn't think he was much out on the pull anymore.

Maybe when he got out of his depressive funk.

Until then he was simply a miserable git to be around.

So I shouldn't introduce Jakob to him just yet.

But Alex was always sweet. If Jakob wanted, I'd introduce them a weekend Alex was home. Maybe even Andreas would come home—I figured Jakob would have an even better time meeting him.

Andreas had a positive outlook on life. He had no issues with his sexuality, no issues being in a relationship with another guy. He was simply *easy*. And easy-going person. Exactly the kind of person Jakob needed right now.

Too bad he was in the army—and I had no idea when he next came home for a visit.

"You really mean it? We can... talk?" He didn't dare look at me.

"I do, Jakob. You can come talk to me anytime, anywhere." He didn't have to be alone with it all. If he needed someone to unload on, I could be there for him.

He nodded with a thoughtful expression on his face. "It's been great talking to you now."

"Good." It had for me too. I'd got answers—and learned more than I ever could've thought possible.

Jakob clearly needed someone to be there for him, since no one but me knew about his struggles.

We hadn't had sex, forced or otherwise, so that was a relief.

Since nothing had happened, nothing was awkward. So I could be his friend.

CHAPTER 8

I should've walked on clouds when I left Burger King, but after the conversation with Jakob had steered in on my dad, I felt rather melancholy and sad.

Had Dad suffered like Jakob did right now? He'd had no one there for him, because Mum had already been dead... He'd had us, obviously, but we'd been too young to understand much.

Christina had understood—but she hadn't realised what the signs meant until after Dad was gone. That still tore at her, but she didn't talk about it much anymore. I didn't tend to bring up our parents either, because it always brought the mood down.

I moved towards the gas station almost on autopilot. I wasn't sure if Roar would be there or not, but the butterflies in my stomach fluttered with hope.

I needed something good right now, after the draining conversation I'd just been involved in.

The only thing I could think about that would cheer me up would be to see him. See his stoic face, the bruise under one eye, the ruffled, dirty-blond hair...

He *was* there.

Right behind the counter, serving a customer.

His gaze cut to the side, over the customer's shoulder, as I walked in, and we stared at each other for several seconds.

Once his customer—the only one in the shop at that moment—left, I walked up to the counter.

"Hey."

"Hi, Maria." He stared at me, all intense and inscrutable. "Are you all right?"

"Mhmm." I wasn't sure this had been a good idea. I had nothing to *say* to him. But seeing him made the butterflies in my stomach go wild.

When had they appeared, even? They hadn't been there Saturday night, or this morning at lunch. But they were there now and they weren't subtle about it.

His brows drew together in a frown. "You don't seem all right."

"Oh." I shook my head a little to clear my thoughts. "I've been at BK. Had a chat with Jakob."

Now his frown *deepened*. "What did he do to you?"

I blinked, then promptly realised he was taking my melancholia as sadness. "Nothing! Nothing at all happened. My virtue's all intact. Such as it is."

Oh my god, can you be more lame?

But his expression cleared, a little at least. He still seemed a bit unsure, sceptical. "How can you be certain he wasn't lying?"

I bit my lower lip. "I can't tell you, but trust me, he wasn't lying." I didn't know Jakob, but even so I could tell the blatant emotions, the fear and the uncertainty and the anxiety, were *real*. "He hasn't hurt me. I didn't do anything to him. It's all good."

He licked his lips. "Then why aren't you happy?"

Good question. "Our conversation touched upon my parents. My dad."

"What's wrong with them?" He leaned on the counter now so he was a bit closer to me.

"They're dead."

"Oh." That drew him up short. "I'm sorry."

"It's okay." I shrugged. "It's years since Mum died, and Dad…" I did a quick calculation in my head. "Huh. It's been four years. Over four years now."

He looked away. "My mum's dead too."

Oh no. "So it's just you and your stepfather?" That tosser.

He nodded. "It's been two years now."

"I'm sorry, Roar." He didn't have anymore bruises on his face, at least. I hoped that meant the old git hadn't beat on him lately.

"It is what it is." He shrugged, then looked down at me. "Still wearing it, huh?"

"Yeah." His hoodie. It was big on me, but it was comfortable. "I like it."

"You can have it if you want." He leaned his arms on the counter, gaze intense as it bore into me.

"I don't want to take your clothes. I'm just borrowing it for a little while." I braced my arms against the counter too, leaning in closer to him. "It made me feel good, when I was freaking out about everything. But now that all's fine I don't really need it anymore."

His gaze searched mine. "You look good in it."

I smiled, but didn't get a chance to answer, because he leaned in all the way and pressed his lips to mine.

I leaned in closer, pressing further into the kiss, wanting to feel more of him. His lips were warm and soft, and when his tongue ran over my bottom lip, I opened my mouth to accept it inside—

The sliding doors *whooshed* open.

We pulled apart and looked around guiltily, but the person who'd come inside didn't so much as glance at us. He walked resolutely over to the fridges, got a frozen pizza and a bottle of Cola, then came up to the counter.

I stepped to the side as Roar rang him up.

The guy left just as silently and resolutely as he'd come in, without so much as a *bye* to Roar.

"Hey, Maria, come over here." Roar motioned with his head to the other side of the counter, past the pastries to where there was space enough for him to come out—and for me to come in.

He took my hand and drew me past the counter, up flush against him.

I put a hand on his stomach as I tilted my head up to meet his kiss.

His hands wrapped around me, all strong and sure and *safe*. People might say Roar was dangerous, but he wasn't to me. To me he'd been nothing but kind and compassionate.

"I like you, Roar," I said when the kiss tapered off.

He swallowed. "I like you too."

The butterflies started up again, going wild in my stomach.

His arms tightened around me, pressing me up even closer to him if that was at all possible.

I hooked my hands around his neck, then brushed my lips over his jaw, feeling the slight stubble there rasp against them.

The sliding doors opened again, this time bringing with them a crowd of rowdy lads.

I stepped away from Roar with regret, and he gave me a small smile I hoped conveyed the same regret.

I glanced over at the lads, they were probably in their early to mid-twenties somewhere. Then I glanced at my phone.

"I have to go home." It was late and there was school in the morning. "I don't know how you manage to work so late and still get up for school, but I need my sleep."

He pressed his lips together, looked away, then gave me another small smile. "I'll see you tomorrow then."

"Yeah." I couldn't wait to see him again. "Sit with me at lunch?"

He nodded. "I will."

"Great." I glanced behind me again. The group of lads were busy perusing the crisps section, so I dared take a step forward and press a light, brief, chaste kiss to Roar's lips. "Tomorrow then."

"Be careful on your way home," he said, watching me intently as I moved away from him.

"I always am."

I left the gas station and followed the main road up past the park where I'd first met Roar on Saturday.

I preferred to follow the main road, as there were always cars out and about. If something were to happen there, there were houses all around too.

This was a small town, but things happened here too. I'd read about women being raped in the paper, or that time someone tried to rob a bus with an axe. Things happened here, as they did everywhere.

Andreas and Alex had been attacked one time they'd been out and taken the shortcut through the marina. Alex had taken an iron bar to the head. Now, *that* was scary.

I never took the route through the marina when it was dark, not after that. Not that that arsehole would come around and gay bash me, considering I wasn't gay and a girl, but still.

It was a place where no one could hear me if I screamed. A place for someone to lurk without me seeing them.

No, it was better to follow the main road.

CHAPTER 9

I looked for Roar as soon as I came to school the morning after, but didn't spot him anywhere outside. Nor did I see Iselin.

Jakob, however, broke off from his group of friends and came over to walk with me towards the double doors.

"Hey."

"Hi." I looked at him expectantly. Did he want to talk now? "You sure you want to be seen with me?" I glanced over at his friends, who all were looking at us.

"Nothing wrong with that, is there?" He seemed in better spirits today, not as sad and anxious and nervous as he had last night.

"No." Still, wouldn't the fact we were actually

talking now fire up the rumours even more? Not that I minded, not *much*, not as long as Roar knew the truth.

"I just wanted to say thanks for last night." He clutched the strap of his shoulder bag tight.

"No problem." I was just happy I'd found out what had happened—or in this case hadn't happened —on Saturday. And I hoped my words had been of some comfort to him, at least.

It seemed they had, as he was a bit more uplifted today.

"What you said last night... I think I've figured it out."

We were inside now, and I stopped in front of the stairs that led up to the general studies classrooms. I was on the ground floor, through the corridor next to the stairs.

"Oh yeah?"

"Yeah." He pursed his lips as he stared intently down at the floor. "I mean, I've known it for a while, but it wasn't in the cards for me... except maybe it is?"

He was rambling. It was a little adorable. If a guy could be adorable. *They definitely can.*

"What is it, Jakob?" I asked, trying not to laugh.

"Teaching."

I raised my eyebrows in wonder. I hadn't seen *that* one coming. "That's not such a bad career, is it?"

"My parents think so." He shrugged awkwardly. "They want me to be a lawyer, or a doctor, or an engineer. But I don't want that."

"Then don't do it." I'd never once been pushed to do something I didn't want. None of us had, our family were so open and supportive with each other.

"I've been up half the night searching online, and I found they've got a really great programme in Trondheim and Volda, not too far from here. In Trondheim they've got an integrated master, so five years of study, but in Volda it's a bachelor."

"The integrated master is for teaching at higher levels, isn't it?" I wasn't that into what kind of education you needed as a teacher, but I knew at least my Norwegian teacher had a master-degree.

He nodded eagerly, excited now, which only proved he should do what he liked instead of what someone else expected. "It is. I want to teach kids, and for that I'd only need a bachelor-degree as well as a year of professional teacher qualification."

"Well, Alex goes to school in Volda. He's taking a year-course in English. It's a good school, from what I've heard."

"Alex?" He gave me a confused look.

"My brother's boyfriend," I clarified. "And his

brother's studying social work, also in Volda. I've heard a lot of great stuff about that school. I'm going to Trondheim to study psychology—if I get in anyway—so if you decide to go there, we'll have to meet up."

He frowned slightly. "Psychology? I thought you were going further with your dancing."

"What makes you think that?"

"Well, since you're doing dance for upper secondary, I just figured." He got all nervous again, which I could tell from the hesitation in his voice to how he stared at the floor.

"I wanted to. Take it further, live off of it. But it's hard, you know? It's a difficult career choice. Besides, I don't enjoy it like I used to. It's fine as a hobby, that way it's fun, but I don't want to make a career out of it." I'd thought long and hard about in the past year. "I want a career where I'm guaranteed a job. Where I won't have to live paycheck to paycheck. A safe job."

And psychology was interesting too.

"I'm applying the minute the fifteenth rolls around."

He chuckled. "You've got until the fifteenth of April to apply. There's no stress."

"I know. I just know what I want and I want to get it over with." I'd had long talks with my uncle during the past year, trying to figure out what I wanted with my life. I had a direction now, and I was going with it.

The bell rang overhead.

"Well, that's my cue." I motioned with my head towards the music, dance, and drama department.

"Yeah." He looked at me, expression more open and happy that I'd seen it before. "I'll see you at lunch?"

"Yeah, sure." Though that would be quite an interesting lunch. If I was going to be at a table with Roar *and* Jakob, not to mention Iselin… That could get awkward.

But I wasn't about to say no either.

I didn't have many friends, and I wasn't about to turn away someone who could become one. Especially not someone as troubled as Jakob. He deserved some good in his life. To be who he was around people who understood.

THE FIRST TWO hours passed quickly, and as soon as we had a fifteen minutes recess, I headed to the girl toilets on the ground floor. There weren't as many people there as the main one upstairs.

I still hadn't seen Roar today, not even in passing

in the halls, and that occupied my thoughts as I washed my hands.

A toilet flushed behind me, but I paid it no mind.

Not until someone loomed up behind me—and I looked up to meet Hedda's angry gaze in the mirror.

"So not only did you sleep with my boyfriend, you're stealing him away too?"

I grabbed some paper to dry my hands, threw it in the rubbish, then turned to face her. "I'm not stealing him away from you."

"You seemed pretty chummy earlier." Her lips, usually painted pink or red, were natural today. They were pressed into a thin, angry line. Her eyes were a little puffy, which told me she'd been crying. Though her mascara seemed mostly intact.

"Chummy? Yeah, we were friendly. We were *talking*. He's nice." I couldn't tell her Jakob's secret, so I wasn't sure if I should even correct her about the whole *sleeping together* thing. She might think she had a chance with him again if she found out he hadn't cheated on her.

"I know he's nice. He's *my* boyfriend!"

"He's not. Not anymore." Jakob had told me himself they'd broken up. "So you've got no claims on him. He can speak to whoever he wants. We're friends."

That was taking it a bit too far, considering we

didn't know each other at all, but I had a feeling we were quickly moving towards friendship.

"Friends don't sleep with friends," she snapped.

I sighed. "If you have a problem, you should take it up with Jakob. This is none of my business."

"It is!" she shrieked, anger overflowing. "You slept with him! You ruined us."

Oh jesus. I did not want to be a part of any of this drama.

"Look Hedda. If your boyfriend cheats on you, there's a problem with *your* relationship. Don't take it out on me." As long as she didn't hit me or pull my hair again, I'd be happy. "You two have problems. I've got no problems with either of you."

"You *wrecked* us." Now she seemed close to crying again. "Why did he sleep with you? I offer myself on a silver platter to him and *nothing*, but you get him in bed. What do you have that I don't?"

She did looked wrecked.

And damn it, but I felt sorry for her. "Nothing. I didn't get him into bed. We slept in the same bed, yes, but we didn't do anything."

She pulled a grimace that clearly said she didn't believe me. "Yeah, right."

"It's true. I swear. Cross my heart." She hadn't asked to fall in love with a closeted gay guy, after all. And considering Jakob wasn't ready to come out, he hadn't told her, and so she had no idea just what the truth was.

She frowned and cocked her head. "You're serious?"

"Yeah." I couldn't tell her anymore, but that I hadn't slept with her boyfriend should be enough. "We didn't have sex. And I'm not interested in Jakob."

She snorted. "You were talking this morning, standing all close and shit. You seemed pretty *interested*, the both of you."

"Friends, Hedda." I flicked my ponytail over my shoulder. "A guy and a girl can be friends without there being anything else between them."

"I don't believe that." She crossed her arms over her chest.

"Well, it's true." The bell rang overhead. "You should get over Jakob."

"What the hell does that mean?" She was on my heels as I exited the toilets. "There *is* something between you, isn't there?"

"No, there isn't."

"Then how do you *know*?"

"Because you broke up." I turned to face her, walking backwards. "Isn't that enough? When you break up it's because you don't want to be together anymore."

"He broke up with *me*."

"He doesn't want to be with you, Hedda." I didn't want to put words in Jakob's mouth, but I knew this much. She wasn't the right gender for him, after all.

I also didn't want her hassling me.

"I've got to go." I didn't want to be late for class again. Yesterday had been more than enough. "Just… get over him."

I left her standing there, seemingly fighting tears.

Even if I felt sorry for her, I wasn't inclined to skip class to comfort her. She'd slapped me, after all, and now she'd harassed me in the bloody toilets.

Yes, breakups hurt—I knew that firsthand, even if I'd been the one who broke up with Magnus last year. We'd been together for seven months though, I'd been used to him, and going from seeing him almost every day to not even talking anymore, had been hard.

Besides, I was better off without him.

Jakob was better off without Hedda.

And she was better off without him—even if she didn't realise it right now. She would eventually.

CHAPTER 10

here the hell is Roar?

The bell had rung for lunch and I didn't see him anywhere. He'd agreed to sit with me at lunch, but I was currently occupying a table with only Iselin for company.

Iselin poured over her religion book. "We've got a two-hour test after lunch," she explained at my raised eyebrows. "And I hardly got to read last night "

"What were you so busy with?"

Iselin lived for school, to get good grades. She wanted to be a veterinarian and thus needed near-perfect grades to get in.

"Mum and Dad had a row, and Mum had a complete meltdown." She shrugged, as if it wasn't a big deal. Which, considering how often it happen lately, it wasn't anymore.

"Are they... okay?" They'd been on the edge of divorce before, but had always managed to stick together through it.

Iselin only shrugged again and bent back over her book.

"Hi, Maria." Jakob sat down next to me.

Iselin's head shot up and she stared at him with wide eyes.

"Hi." Jakob smiled shyly at her, which caused Iselin to blush and look back down at her book.

"Don't mind her, she's stressed about a test she's got after lunch." I turned to him. "So I had a run-in with Hedda earlier."

"What did she have to say?" he asked in trepidation. "She didn't attack you again, did she?"

I shook my head. "I think she just wanted answers."

"To what?" He honestly seemed confused.

"Well, she asked me what I had that she didn't."

He blinked. "Uhh..."

"I didn't say anything. Well, not about *that*. But I did tell her we haven't slept together." I saw Iselin glance up at me from the corner of my eye, but I kept my focus on Jakob.

He bit his lip guiltily. "I kind of told her we had, to get her off my back."

I snorted a laugh. "Jesus."

"I'm sorry."

"Hey, it's okay—" Something drew my attention. Several people were standing at the windows, clearly looking at something down in the schoolyard. "What's going on over there?"

"Don't know." Jakob leant forwards so he could look past me.

Voices filtered over to us, broken words that I couldn't make out to full sentences.

"A fight?" He rose halfway. "Someone's fighting outside."

Something heavy settled in my stomach.

Roar had said we'd see each other at lunch, but he wasn't here. He was known for getting in trouble, known for fighting, and now there was a fight outside—

"Shit." I was up off my chair and out of the cafeteria before the other two could blink.

I ran down the stairs, trying my best not to trip and fall down them, then jumped the last two. Once I pushed the doors open, I saw a gang of lads gathered out there.

I couldn't see what they were gathered around, but I had a sick feeling in my stomach.

They yelled, words I couldn't make out in my panic as I hurried forwards. I pushed past them, and many of them gave me odd looks, but I got into the ring.

And I was right.

It was Roar.

And some other arsehole—one of Jakob's friends.

"Roar!"

His head whipped around to stare at me—but I shouldn't have yelled, because the other guy's fist connected with Roar's face, bringing him to his knees.

Roar glanced up at me briefly, jaw set, and eyes dark, then he turned and tackled the other guy to the ground.

"Roar, no!"

Why was he fighting one of Jakob's friends?

I wanted to stop them, but I had nothing on two grown-up lads in a fistfight. I didn't want to see Roar hurt, and the fist he'd taken to the face earlier had seemed to *really hurt*.

Other people moved into the circle now too—and finally broke the two of them apart.

Jakob was there, pushing his friend back and talking to him in a low voice.

Someone I didn't know held Roar back, but he

struggled in the guy's grip, eyes only for the one he'd been fighting.

"Roar?" I stepped up in front of him, not quite blocking his view over to Jakob and his friend, but I got his attention.

His expression softened the tiniest bit and he stopped struggling against the guy who held him back. The guy slowly let him go, seemingly unsure if it was wise or not.

I stepped up closer to Roar to look at his face. He still had the black eye his stepfather had given him, and I could see some red swelling on his cheekbone on the other side.

"Shit." Not only did he have to endure violence at home, but he had to at school too. "What happened?"

He pressed his lips together and glared over my shoulder. "He said something I disagreed with."

I glanced over my shoulder too, but there was no answers there, so I turned back to frown up at Roar. "You can't go around and hit everyone you disagree with—"

He turned dark eyes on me. "He said some pretty nasty shit about *you*."

That brought me up short. "Oh."

"Yeah." He ran a hand through his hair, messing it up.

I looked over my shoulder again. Jakob was still

conversing in low tones to his friend, who seemed to be arguing his case.

The circle of people that had been gathered when the fight was ongoing now slowly dissipated. I could see Iselin hovering near the doors, but Roar was more important right now.

"Are you, like, defending my honour?" I tried for teasing, but it didn't seem to lighten his mood any.

"I'm not going to stand by and listen while some arsehole call you a slag." He clenched his teeth so hard a muscle in his jaw ticked.

That was a kick to the gut.

A slag? Really?

I didn't bother looking behind me again. It was all probably because of Saturday night, and then because Jakob had told a small lie to Hedda to get her off her back.

"I'm not, you know." I couldn't care less about anyone else, but what he thought about me was the most important thing in the world right now.

"I know." His gaze was inscrutable as he looked down at me. "People just like to talk shit. They do about me all the time."

And I'd heard a lot of it and taken it to heart. That he was dangerous…

He wasn't! He could've simply walked away, not got involved, but he'd heard someone say something bad about me and he'd dealt with it. Perhaps not in the right way, but he'd dealt with it the only way he knew how.

The bell rang.

"Damn bell," I murmured. "It always ruins my conversations lately." I took another step closer to him. If I took just one more, our bodies would be so close we'd press up together. As it was, I only reached out to splay my hand over his stomach. "When are you done with your last class today?"

"At three."

"Do you have any plans afterwards?"

Please don't have any plans!

He shook his head, gaze searching my face.

"I'll wait for you, then. We can talk? Spend time together?"

He nodded now. "That sounds good."

"Great." I smiled at him, my gaze zeroing in on his lips. I'd kissed those lips last night and I wanted to do it again—but not in a schoolyard that was still full of people. They were slowly trickling inside, though.

Iselin still stood by the doors, jumping slightly up and down on her feet. She had one rucksack dangling from both of her shoulders.

"I have to go." I took his hand in mine and

squeezed. His knuckles were red and sore. "See you later then?"

He only nodded, but kept hold of my hand as I stepped back. Our arms rose, stretched out, and then we had to let go.

I cast him one last, longing look before I turned to Iselin and relieved her of my bag.

She glanced at Roar, who still hadn't moved from the spot he'd been standing in. "You and Roar?"

"Yeah," I said as I held the door open for her.

She slipped inside and I followed close behind her.

"*Roar*, of all people." She seemed shocked, like she couldn't believe I'd ever be interested in someone like him.

I didn't have time to say anything else, to correct her skewered opinion of him. "See you tomorrow, okay?" I didn't want her to wait for me after school, not when I was seeing Roar after.

As for the rest of the evening... I didn't know what that would entail, but I hoped there'd be a lot of Roar in it.

CHAPTER 11

I had two hours to kill until Roar finished for the day, and I found an empty room to practice in. Since the room belonged to us in music, dance, and drama department, it had a stereo —and I plugged in my phone.

Once the music reverberated through the room, I started moving to it.

Our last class of the day had been dance, so I was still in my gear. A tight leotard and knee-short tights today. I didn't bother with the shoes, as it was easier to keep my footing when I was barefoot.

Dancing on my own—or with Nik—was always what I preferred. I didn't have to focus on other people, on having perfect technique, I could simply lose myself in the music and in the dance.

And I did.

I didn't know how long I was immersed in my own world. All I knew was that the songs ended and blended into a new one, and I danced exactly like how I wanted, without incorporating anyone else's choreography into it.

At one point, I spun around in a pirouette, and my gaze passed over the door— and Roar stood there.

I spun to a halt, almost losing my balance in surprise.

"It's not been two hours yet," I said dumbly.

He chuckled and came further into the room. "The teacher had to leave. Something about a sick child."

"Oh." I watched him come closer, nervous and excited all at once. The kiss from last night flashed through my mind—and I wanted it again.

"You're a great dancer." His gaze travelled down my body, and his eyes were intense as they took me in.

I should feel self-conscious, considering my tight dancing gear didn't hide much, but I *didn't*.

It only made me feel more confident—knowing that he liked what he saw.

"Do you know anything about dance?"

He gave a guilty laugh. "No. But the way you move—"

I took the few steps separating us, hooked my arms around his neck, and leaned up to press my lips to his, effectively shutting him up.

His arms slid around my waist, tightening and pulling me up close. He wore jeans and his leather jacket open over a hoodie almost identical to the one he'd given me.

He felt so good against me, all warm and hard and strong.

If we hadn't been in school, I would've dragged him off to the nearest bed. That's how much I wanted him— and it was weird, because I didn't actually *know* him.

Last year, it had taken me months to put out for my ex, and after insistent pouting from him, I eventually did. Roar hadn't even hinted at sex and here I was, craving it.

"Do you have to work tonight?" I asked eventually, drawing back from our kiss.

"I've got Tuesday's off."

I slid one hand up his neck, over his jaw, ear, and into his hair. "Can you go home?"

He shook his head.

"Come home with me then." I stared into his eyes, willing him to say yes.

"You sure?" He stared just as intently back.

"Yeah." I pressed another kiss to his lips. "I think my uncle's at work, so we can order take-away. Get it delivered straight to my front door." I toyed with a few strands of his hair.

He bowed his head a little. "That does sound nice."

"All right then." I stepped out of his arms and went over to unplug my phone and shrug into his hoodie. I pulled a pair of joggers from my rucksack over my tights, because otherwise I'd freeze to death when I got outside. Then I grabbed my rucksack, put it over one shoulder, and turned to look at him. "You coming?"

He smiled slightly, nodded, and we walked out side by side. He had a bag thrown over his shoulder.

"Has your step-dad always been a mean bastard?" I asked, then cursed myself for using such crass words. Maybe Roar cared for him, even if he hit him.

"Pretty much." He glanced briefly at me. "He wasn't so bad before Mum died though. It was after he started drinking excessively—and got more violent the more he drank."

"Doesn't he work?" He had to get money for alcohol from someplace.

"He's on welfare." Roar sighed. "So he's always

home, and he use all his money on beer and Vodka. Ever since this year started I've contemplating dropping out." He swallowed audibly. "That way I could get a better job, a full-time one, and move out on my own. But I don't want to work in a bloody gas station for the rest of my life, so I decided to stick it out another year."

"You want to do higher education?" I could see how it'd be hard to find a job that paid for a flat and all the bills that brought with it, when he spent every single day at school.

He nodded. "Not quite sure what I want to do. All I know is I don't want to be stuck in this town, working at the gas station or the supermarket. Still got over a month to think about it, though, so I've got time."

"You'll figure it out." I sounded confident. "And if you don't, you've got time to try and fail a little."

He cast me a wry look. "Do you know what you're going to do?"

"Yep. I'm going to Trondheim to study psychology. I've got a good enough average to get in, as long as I don't completely mess up my exams so they pull my average down."

"I figured you'd do more with your dancing."

"Why does everyone say that?" I exclaimed, but I laughed as I did.

"Isn't that what you people want? If you take music, dance, or drama during upper secondary, you tend to want to pursue a career in it?"

"Well, I don't. I love to dance, I do, but I want it to stay fun. I don't want it to be my job. I don't want to struggle for the rest of my life. I want a job that pays well, where I know I can get a full-time position. One that I don't have to worry about."

He nodded. "That's a good choice."

"I know." I smiled to myself.

All Ben had ever wanted was to live off music, but he currently worked as a bartender. Nik was down in Oslo, studying dance at the Bårdar Academy—and I didn't doubt he'd succeed, but he had to work hard for it.

I didn't want dance to be a job. Dance was fun. And it wouldn't be if I was required to do it to be able to live and pay my bills.

"What do you do all day when you can't go home?" I asked, wanting to change the subject back to him. I wanted to know *everything* about him.

"Whatever I can." He tilted his head back to stare up at the cloudy sky. "I stay back at school to do homework. I go out to eat, either at BK or one of the many take-away places around town. I go in early to work, spend some time in the back room. I go for walks. Whatever I can to avoid him."

I frowned down at the ground. It wasn't fair that he should live like that. "That's messed up, Roar."

"I know. But there's only a few months left now until school's over, and as soon as I get in somewhere. I'm gone."

That made me feel bad, even though it shouldn't. I didn't know him—I didn't have any right to him. And considering how his life was, of course he'd want to get away. I would've too.

The house was locked when we came there, which meant Thomas was indeed at work. If Ben was in or not was a guessing game, but he wasn't on the ground floor anyway.

"What does your uncle do?" He looked around with interest.

"He's a doctor. Works at the hospital."

"Has he got any children?" He stopped to look at our school pictures that hung on the walls in the staircase.

"No, none of his own. He's taken care of my cousin Ben for most of his life. His mum's dead. And then when our dad… died… he took us in too."

"Who's *us*?" He looked at me with interest.

"Me, I'm the youngest, and my older brother and sister. Andreas and Christina." I pointed them out in each their picture. "Christina's moved out with her boyfriend. Andreas' in the army, but his boyfriend

Alex comes back here during the weekends." I couldn't show him a picture of Alex, because he wasn't in any of them. He hadn't been in Andreas' class.

"You're lucky to have someone who takes all of you in." He gazed at my school picture from seventh grade.

"That's Thomas. He took Alex in too, last year. His parents are shitty. And after his brother celebrated Christmas with us, he comes back here most weekends too with Alex."

He looked like he couldn't quite believe it. "And your uncle doesn't mind? All those people..."

"No, I think he likes it." I smiled. "Uncle's great. He's done so much for all of us. He's the only one in the family—in his generation and above, anyway—who we keep in contact with."

"The rest of your family's bad?"

"Well... yeah. Grandma's okay, but she lives in Spain, so it's not often we get to see her. My dad's dead, Ben's mum's dead, and my uncle's oldest brother... he's not around. No one wants him around either." I didn't like to think about him and how Jo and Jørgen had suffered through their entire childhood.

If Thomas had known what had been going on there, I was pretty sure he would've taken them both in too. But they'd kept themselves separated from the rest of the family, so Jo and Jørgen had suffered without anyone being the wiser.

"So it's not all good in my family either. In fact, some things are pretty bad." I led him up the stairs. "That's my uncle's bedroom." It was the door to the right. "There's the bathroom, and that's Christina's old room that's usually Leo's now, and at the end of the hall… my room." I opened the door and preceded him inside.

I wished I'd cleaned it better that morning, because clothes and books were scattered around.

Then again, I hadn't known I'd bring Roar home earlier today.

I dropped my rucksack next to my desk. He tentatively took a seat on the chair, whereas I sat on the edge of my bed.

His foot kept tapping now he sat down, like he was nervous.

Maybe he is.

"Are you hungry now?" Considering he'd been outside fighting during lunch, I didn't reckon he'd had anything to eat then.

He shrugged.

"Have you had anything to eat today?" I raised both eyebrows questioningly.

"No," he admitted, voice low.

"Right then." I dragged my laptop over and opened it. Once I typed in my password, my browser with all its tabs came up on the screen.

I typed in the URL for my favourite take-away shop, then turned it around to hand him the laptop. "Figure out what you want and I'll ring and order."

He took the laptop almost hesitantly, but did as I said.

As he went through the menu I took my phone up from my pocket. Or his, considering the hoodie was technically his.

I had several messages.

Iselin: Have you left school?

Never mind, I just saw you leave with Roar.

Roar, really? When did that happen? You have to tell me everything!

And Jakob? Where does he fit?

Maria… answer your damn messages!

I smiled as I scrolled through and read all of her six texts. She did deserve an explanation though, she was my best friend after all, but not by text and not *now*.

Right now I had other, more important things on my mind.

I glanced up at Roar, whose gaze was trained on my laptop. His thumb traced his bottom lip as he read.

Yeah, I've definitely got more important things going on right now.

CHAPTER 12

I ran down to pay for the food once the doorbell rang, leaving Roar surfing on my laptop. Now he had access to one with stable internet, he'd instantly started searching colleges and universities to see what they had to offer.

I carried the plastic bag with the take-out containers into the kitchen, where I gathered seasoning for the chips, ketchup, cutlery, glasses, and drinks. We only had a bottle of Solo, so it would have to do.

It was too much for me to carry in one go, so I grabbed a plastic bag from under the sink where I put everything in. That way I only had to carry two bags upstairs.

Once out in the hall, I stopped with one foot on the stairs.

Roar's in my room. We're spending the evening together.

Maybe even the night.

I need to be prepared.

I sat the bags on that first step, then turned and hurried down to the basement. Since I knew neither Andreas nor Alex were home, I went into their room.

Surely they'd have some spare condoms lying around?

I searched through Andreas' bedside table drawer, but only found a half-empty bottle of lube and some magazines with naked girls on front.

"Really, Andreas?" I stared down at the one on top. He was in a relationship with Alex. Did he need magazines with naked girls on them? Then again, those magazines did have interesting articles in them, so it wasn't like they were *porn*. Not completely anyway.

There were no condoms, which was weird, because I knew they had sex.

Maybe they do it bare.

Easy for them; they don't have to worry about unwanted pregnancies.

I drew a deep breath as I closed the bedroom door after me, then I walked over to knock on Ben's. If he was home I had to confess what I needed—better than have bare sex—and take the embarrassment that would lead to.

But Ben didn't answer, and when I cracked his bedroom door open, his room was empty.

And Ben had condoms. Heaps of them.

"Thanks, Ben." I grabbed three from the stash he had in his drawer. Considering how many there were, I didn't think he'd miss the few I took. Or stole, but condoms from my cousin wasn't the worst thing I could've stolen.

I stuffed the condoms in my pockets, ran back upstairs, grabbed the two bags, and hightailed it up to my room.

Roar still sat on my desk chair with my laptop propped on his knees. He looked up as I came in.

"Dinner's been delivered." I didn't have much space for eating though. It was either the desk or the bed.

Andreas and Ben had bigger rooms than I had, with sofas and TVs. I only had my bed, desk, and several bookshelves.

I opted to sit on the bed, scooting up so I rested my back against the wall.

Roar watched me silently as I sat the take-away containers out, then took out cutlery that I lay atop

113

them, and poured soda into two glasses that I put on each bedside table.

"Come on." I patted the bed next to me.

He glanced from the empty space to me and back again, but then he put the laptop on the desk and came to sit besides me.

Our shoulders pressed together as we sat down to eat, but whereas he again seemed nervous, I only felt content. Content... and excited. Because who knew what would happen once we'd finished dinner?

"How was your mum, Roar?" I asked, just as much to try and put him at ease as to get my thoughts out of the gutter.

"She was nice. A gentle person. I don't know how she managed to keep up with my step-dad, but she did. Other than that, she was perfect." He smiled slightly as he talked about her. "She loved me. But she also loved him, something I can't understand. He hit her. Not that often, but when they fought, it got dirty. He never hit me though, not back when she was alive."

"That only came after?" I felt so sorry for him.

"Yeah. If she'd known... I don't think she would've left me in his care if she had."

"How did she die?"

He swallowed audibly, emotional now. "Aneurism."

"Shit. I'm sorry." I cut my chicken fillets up into small pieces. "Didn't you have any other family? What about your biological dad?"

"He's never been in the picture. He was a sailor and whenever they docked here, he'd get together with my mum. But he had a wife and kids back home."

I blinked. "So you've got siblings you've never met?"

"Yeah." He shook his head. "It doesn't matter. He knew she got pregnant and never bothered to come back. That's all I need to know about *him*. Then my mum married my stepfather and that was that."

"My dad couldn't live without Mum. He managed, for a few years, but then… yeah."

He stared down at his food. "Sometimes I think that's the case with my stepfather too. Before Mum died, he had a good job, he only drank on weekends, he could laugh and be fun to be around. But once she was gone… he changed completely."

"So you loved him once?"

He nodded. "He resents being stuck with me now."

"Has he told you that?" My heart bled for him.

"Yep. In those exact words."

We fell silent after that. I didn't know what to say,

and he likely didn't want to talk about his stepfather anymore.

So we ate our food, sitting in loaded, but also sort of comfortable, silence.

He finished before me, and he folded the box back together and put it in the bag. Then he leaned back to stare up at the ceiling until I finished and followed his example.

I had to lean over him to get the bag from the floor, and then again as I put it back down with my take-away box added in there atop his.

I put a hand on his chest, bracing myself, then chanced a quick glance up at him.

He stared at me, face unreadable, but his brown eyes swirling with emotion.

"Roar..." I took a chance before I could second-guess myself and sat up to straddle his lap. Then I bent forward to kiss him.

He ran his hands up my arms, over my shoulders, and down my back, where he settled them on the small of my back.

I pressed down closer to him—and he took the hint. His hands moved further down, over my bum, and gripping my thighs.

Then he flipped us around so I was the one on my back and he was the one atop me.

I wrapped my arms around his neck, holding him

down, refusing to let him ease off me. He wasn't too heavy, not yet anyway. In fact, having his weight press me into the mattress felt *good*.

"Hey, Maria?" he asked, lips hovering close to mine.

"Hmm?" I needed him to kiss me again. We'd talked a lot earlier, now it was time for *this*.

"Maybe this isn't such a good idea?"

"This is a *great* idea." I hooked one leg over his hips.

He squirmed uncomfortably—and he moved so that I felt exactly *why* he was uncomfortable.

I smiled against his lips, nipping on his bottom one. "Don't you want to do this?"

"Oh, trust me I do."

"Then what's the problem?"

"I don't want to force you into anything."

That brought me up short. "Does it look like I'm being forced?" I stared at him. "I want this so much I'm about to force *you* if you don't hurry up and get with the plan."

He gave a startled laugh. "I'm with the plan. It's just I don't have anything. Protection, I mean."

"That's okay. I do." I reached into my pocket and drew out the three brightly coloured condom packets.

Roar eyed them incredulously. "Have you been going around with those in your pocket all day?"

"No." It was my turn to laugh. "I stole them from my cousin when I went down to get the food. Don't worry, he won't miss them, he's got a whole stash."

For a minute he seemed embarrassed , but then he smiled widely—before he crushed his lips to mine.

I moved my hands down to slip under his hoodie and T-shirt, and once I encountered his bare skin, he followed suit. I still wore my leotard though, so even when he unzipped the hoodie, he was met with only stretchy material.

"Dammit." I should've changed after my dance-class.

He chuckled.

I unzipped *his* hoodie and slid it off his shoulders. Once it was off, I pulled his T-shirt up.

He sat up on his knees, grabbed the tee, and pulled it off in one quick movement.

I stared at his naked torso, taking in the fading bruises over one side of his ribs. I sat up too and ran my fingers feather-light over the discoloured skin.

"Is this from your stepfather too?"

He stared down at himself. "Yeah."

"What about today? Did he hit you anywhere but your face?" He still had a red mark on his cheek-bone, and it was redder now than it'd been after the fight. He'd probably get a bruise there too by tomorrow.

"He hit me once in the stomach, but not that hard." He traced a circle around the spot he'd been hit.

I let my hand fall down his skin until I met the hem of his boxers. I moved my fingers lower, to grip the fly of his jeans.

He sucked in a breath, but stayed quiet as I unzipped and pulled the jeans down his thighs. His boxers were tight, and in them, clearly outlined, was his dick.

I licked my lips, then looked up at him.

He stared back. "Are you absolutely sure?"

"Oh yeah." I'd never been surer of anything in my *life*.

"Considering what you've just been through, what could've happened to you—"

"Nothing happened. I'm good. Besides, I'm not drunk now. And you're not someone who would sexually assault me."

I threw my feet over the edge of the bed so I could be rid of my joggers. I had to take my tights off too to get my leotard off.

"Are you about to give me a striptease?" he asked teasingly.

I glanced over my shoulder at him. He still sat on

the bed, with his jeans halfway down his thighs. "Would you like that?"

He licked his lips, eye going darker, which told me all I needed to know.

It was weird how I wasn't embarrassed at all. If this had been last year, with my ex, I never stood in front of him to strip. We would've had sex in the dark.

But Roar... there was something special about Roar.

So I inched my tights down, stepped out of them, then pulled the straps on my leotard off my shoulders. All the while, Roar's gaze was glued to me—and nothing made me feel better than to see the desire in his eyes, as well as the hard dick still kept in place by his boxers.

I slid the leotard down and off in one fluid motion, leaving me standing there in only my panties.

"Your turn." I needed him to get naked before I stripped off all the way, so I was a little embarrassed after all.

He stared at my tits.

I looked down too. They were quite small, to the point I was almost flat. I hardly ever needed bras to keep them in check. I liked them small, it was so much better to dance with a nearly flat chest than to have big, flappy ones attached.

I knew guys generally liked bigger tits though, and for a minute I worried my lower lip.

Roar moved, standing up on the floor, and pulling off his jeans and boxers in one move. His dick slapped hard and leaking against his lower stomach.

"And you." His eyes were so intense. They drew me in.

I pushed my panties down over my arse and let them fall to the floor, then I stepped out of them.

Roar took my hand and pulled me flush up close to him.

I hooked my arms around his shoulders, and when he reached down to slide his hands under my thighs, lifting me, I wrapped my legs around his hips.

He turned us around and we fell onto the bed. It bounced a little as our combined weight hit the mattress.

He was all hard planes and muscles, so warm I didn't even feel the chill in my room. He enveloped me, pressed me down, and it was *so good*.

I could definitely get used to this.

CHAPTER 13

*H*is fingers teased me, and I arched my back as one slipped inside me. I was pretty sure I moaned too, because it was him, his finger inside me, and I was so *wet*.

I wanted him so much.

Wanted more than just his fingers. I wanted *all of him.*

"Roar." I fumbled over my head for the condoms but only encountered bunched sheets.

"Impatient?" He grinned at me, nipping at my bottom lip.

"Yeah." I wasn't even ashamed to admit it because it was so true.

He chuckled, produced one of the brightly lit packets, and ripped it open with his teeth.

"Smooth." I laughed, albeit breathlessly.

"I know, right?" He took the slippery condom out, threw the packet away, then reached down in-between us to roll it on himself.

I stared down, watching as he covered his flushed cock with the not-quite-transparent condom.

This is it.

I spread my thighs wider to accommodate him. It'd been awhile since the last time I'd had sex, and I tensed a little in trepidation as he positioned himself against me, head nudging my opening.

"You sure?" He looked down at me, gaze questioning.

"Y-yeah." I was—I wanted this, wanted *him*.

He pressed in and I stopped breathing for a second. *I've forgotten what it feels like, to be filled like this, to have someone else inside me.*

But oh God, it's good!

I moved my pelvis against him, needing more, needing movement and stimulation.

He gave it to me as he set up a steady rhythm.

When he bent down to kiss me, I ran my hands up his neck and over his hair, loving the feel of him against me.

I hiked my feet up to hook them around his waist. His hands cupped the back of my thighs, keeping them in that position, as he thrust harder into me.

I'd always had a hard time orgasming, but that didn't mean sex couldn't be good. Amazing, even, like it was now.

I moaned, eyes falling closed as I lost myself to the pleasure of him moving inside me. It'd been a little tight at first, but now it felt just right. I was wet and he glided in easily, rubbing against me.

He groaned, and I sucked on his bottom lip.

His hips stuttered, then thrust even harder before he buried himself deep and froze.

I clung to his shoulders through his orgasm, running my lips over the thin skin on his neck, tongue lapping at it, sucking.

"Oh fuck." He rolled off me to land at my side.

I slowly stretched my legs out—they were slightly cramped.

He removed the condom, dropped it into the take-away bag on the floor, then fell back down on the bed again. He turned his head on the pillow to look at me, stretching his arm out.

I smiled and rolled in close, resting against him, and he folded his arm around my shoulders.

His chest had a small scattering of hair, darker than the blond hair on his head, and I ran my hand over it, teasing his nipples a little.

His breath came in heavy puffs, chest rising and falling quickly.

But so did mine, so we were in the same boat, as it were.

That was good sex. So much better than it ever was with Magnus.

"It's only been three days." I ran a finger around his nipple, thoughtful.

"Hmm?"

"Three days. Since we met." I tilted my head upwards on his chest so I could look up at his face. "It feels so much longer."

"Yeah." He sighed and closed his eyes. "It does."

I scooted up so I could kiss him. I'd planned on just that one kiss, but it led to two, three, and suddenly I was on my back again with him halfway atop me.

His hand ran over my chest, over the small nubs that were my tits, up to my neck, which he cupped in his palm as he ran his tongue over my bottom lip.

I opened to it, welcoming it in.

I didn't know how long we kissed, I didn't even know how long we'd had sex. It could've been minutes or hours for all knew. And I didn't care. All I wanted was to lie here in bed with him.

When he rolled onto his back again I took notice of how he had a hard time keeping his eyes open.

"Go to sleep, Roar." I pressed in close to his side. "You need it."

"I don't want to be one of those guys who just rolls over and goes to sleep afterwards."

"You're not," I assured him, petting his stomach. "But you don't get much sleep, and I've got this whole bed right here."

"You don't want me to leave?"

"Are you mental? No." I wanted him to stay right where he was, preferably forever, but tonight would do fine too. "Sleep. Relax. You're safe here. If you want to sleep until morning, you can. I'll wake you for school, but other than that I'll leave you alone."

He let out a breath. "You're pretty great, you know that?" He tilted my head up and bent his down, pressing our lips together in a soft kiss.

"I try my best." I grinned. "But you are too, you know. If you hadn't been there on Saturday, I don't know what I would've done."

He stared into my eyes. "I'm glad I was there on Saturday."

"So am I." Now I kissed him, but just a quick, chaste one, before I pushed him away. "Sleep, Roar. I'll be right here."

After another lingering look at me, he did turn over onto his side, with his back to me. I lay down close, wrapping an arm around his waist, and simply listening to him breathe.

He fell asleep rather quickly, which told me all I

needed to know. He did need sleep—and he needed it in a proper bed where no abusive stepfather was around.

It was too early for me to sleep, so I got up eventually. I dressed, went to the toilet to pee—I did not want a UTI—then wandered downstairs.

I heard the TV and ventured into the living room to find Ben sprawled on the sofa.

"Hey. Why're you up here?" He had a TV in his bedroom, after all.

He glanced up at me. "You want to watch something?"

I shook my head, then stared down at him as I stopped next to the sofa. He seemed to be in just as bad a mood as he'd been for a while now. "You all right, Ben?"

"Yeah," he murmured, expression anything but.

I didn't believe him. I also knew I shouldn't push him, because it would only make it worse. I didn't want him to bitch at me.

So I got a glass of water and headed back up to my room.

Roar was in the same position I'd left him in, fast asleep, and I smiled to myself.

Three days in and I was already half-way in love with him. It was unbelievable, incredible, *astonishing*. It shouldn't be possible—except it was. We had a connection, an instant one that had been there ever since he first talked to me Saturday night.

My phone vibrated, and I grabbed it before the sound of it against the bedside table could wake Roar.

I didn't just have the one message, but several. Not from Iselin this time, but for Jakob.

Hedda keeps ringing me. I don't know what to do. She wants to get back together. But I can't, so I'm not answering.

I feel like such a shitty person.

Maria?

So Hedda hadn't taken any of what I'd told her to heart then. *It figures.*

I took a seat on my desk chair, leaving my entire bed to Roar so I wouldn't disturb him, and set to answering Jakob.

Me: *I'm here. You're not a shitty person. She needs to take a hint. Maybe you should just tell her the truth?*

Jakob: *I can't do that. She's vindictive. She'll tell everyone.*

Me: Then she's definitely not worth your time. Don't feel bad about it. That she can't accept your decision is her problem, not yours.

Jakob was such a nice guy, I could understand why she'd want to keep him. But he'd broken up with her, so he wasn't hers to keep anymore. Not that he ever had be, as he wasn't a possession.

Jakob: Do you want to meet up? BK maybe?

Me: I can't. Got a visitor.

Jakob: Oh. OK. Later maybe?

Me: They're staying the right. Rain-check though? Tomorrow, maybe?

Roar had only said he had Tuesdays off, so I took that to mean he had to work again tomorrow.

Jakob: Yeah, OK. That sounds good. See you at school tomorrow then?

Me: Yeah, see you!

I even added on a smiley face to the end of that message, though I wasn't that good at using them normally. Jakob deserved it though, for being such a good, sweet guy.

He gave me a thumps up and that was that.

Iselin next then. She deserved some explanations.

Hey, babe! Sorry, couldn't answer, was busy.

She was active on Facebook, so she saw my message instantly. I stared at the three periods that signalled that she was typing, waiting for the answer.

Iselin: *Busy with Roar?*

Me: *Yeah.*

Iselin: *Is he with you now? Or can I come over?*

Me: *He's here. Sleeping. He needs some proper sleep.*

Iselin: *???*

Me: *He works a lot of nights. Don't get much sleep. So I let him borrow my bed.*

Iselin: YOUR *bed? Wow. Roar? Really… So what's the deal? Are you together?*

I lifted my gaze to stare at his bare back. We hadn't talked about our relationship status yet, but I knew what I wanted.

Me: *I don't know. Maybe.*

Iselin: *Have you slept with him?*

I didn't know what to answer to that. My thumbs hovered over the keyboard on my phone, unsure what to say next. Should I admit it? Deny it? Be vague about it? Be vague about it was the same as admitting it though.

Iselin: *OMG. You have! You slag. Of all the people in school, why Roar? Everyone says he's dangerous, you know.*

Me: *I know, you've told me before. And it felt right. He's great.*

Iselin: *You do know there's some rumours flying around he's on drugs?*

Me: I don't care about rumours. They're hardly ever true. Just look and Jakob and me. Those rumours weren't true either.

Iselin: Are you absolutely sure?

Me: Yeah. I believe him.

Iselin: Are you sure someone else didn't do something to you?

Me: What do you mean?

Iselin: You blacked out... We only had cider. Who gave you something stronger to drink? And did they give you something else with the drink?

Me: Iselin...

Iselin: I'm afraid you were drugged, Maria. It's not normal to get a blackout from cider! You disappeared on me, found something else to drink that gave you a total blackout. I'm afraid you were roofied.

Shit. I hadn't thought about that. Who *had* given me something to drink?

I clicked out of my message with Iselin and pressed Jakob's name.

Hey, about that party on Saturday... Do you know who gave me drinks?

I bit down on my lower lip as I watched the three periods, anxiously awaiting the answer. My phone vibrated with a new message from Iselin, but I had to see what Jakob answered before I could check.

Jakob: Umm, no? Sorry. I was pretty drunk myself. Why?

Me: No, I was just wondering. So it wasn't you?

Jakob: No, you were already pissed when I met you.

Which explained why I didn't remember meeting him—or snogging him—at all.

I clicked in to check what Iselin had written.

Iselin: Maria? I didn't mean to freak you out... I just know that when you were with me, you didn't drink anything but cider.

Me: Jakob didn't give me anything. I just asked. He said I was already drunk by the time we hooked up.

Iselin: Shit.

Me: Who was at that party anyway?

Iselin: I don't know. Lots of people we didn't know. Lots of people from the vocational school, I think. But also from ours. I think Jasmin was there?

Jasmin, a friend of Hedda's... So that was probably where Hedda had heard about Jakob and I.

Dammit, dammit, dammit.

I guess I have to talk to her tomorrow then.

Oh joy.

CHAPTER 14

J woke up before my alarm, all warm and naked and pressed up against Roar's back.

He was still asleep, another testament to just how much he needed his sleep.

I slid out of bed as quietly as I could so I didn't wake him, and tip-toed out of the room to take a shower.

My impending meeting with Jasmin weighed on me—if she was even willing to talk to me. She was Hedda's best friend, surely she'd think I was just as much a home wrecker as Hedda thought.

The warm water was good, and I took meticulous care with the shaving. Not that there was much to shave, considering I always took care with it, but I took it extra careful so I didn't cut myself.

Sex with Roar…

It had been amazing.

I hadn't had sex since Magnus—but Roar was in another category all together. For one thing he didn't pester me constantly about it, and he didn't care only for his own pleasure and comfort.

Roar had worried about me, if he was too heavy, if it had hurt, and afterwards he'd cuddled me.

It had been a much better experience with Roar, yes. And I wanted more. *Much more.*

I finished my shower, wrapped myself up in a towel, wrapped my hair in a towel. Since I hadn't brought any clothes with me into the bathroom, I had to go back into my room like this.

Roar had turned onto his back in my absence, his head turned away from me, but he was clearly still asleep.

"Roar?" It was about time to get up, if he wanted to take a shower before school too. "Roar?" I put a knee on the bed and reached down to shake his shoulder.

He tried to roll away.

"So you're clearly not a morning person." I chuckled as I reached out to grip his shoulder again.

He sat up straight at the same time as his hand locked around my wrist, twisting it.

I gasped in both surprise and pain. "Roar?"

He blinked himself into consciousness, slowly turned his head to stare at me, then he dropped his grip on my wrist as if he'd been burned. "Maria, I'm sorry."

"It's okay." I massaged my wrist and his gaze followed my movements. "Honestly, it's fine." It had only hurt when he'd grabbed hold and twisted, but it was fine now. A dull ache, but it slowly subsided.

He dropped his head into his hands. "What time is it? How long have I been asleep?"

"It's morning. We've got school in an hour." I sat down on the bed. "I figured you'd want a shower before we left?"

He lowered his hands slowly, finally taking in my appearance. "Yeah, I'd like that."

"Does your stepfather attack you when you're sleeping?" I asked, because nothing else could explain his reaction to being shaken awake.

"It's been known to happen," he muttered as he leant over the edge of the bed to search for his clothes.

No wonder he'd slept so long. He could never relax when he finally got to sleep at home.

"Go take a shower. The towels are in the cabinet under the sink."

I tried not to watch as he threw the duvet away to pull on his boxers, but I couldn't help but sneak a peak. And really, we'd had *sex*, there was no harm in seeing him naked the morning after.

He pulled on his jeans too, but left his upper body bare as he grabbed his bag and slipped out of the room.

Is it just me or was this slightly awkward?

I sighed and headed over to my closet, hoping it wouldn't continue to be awkward between us once he came back.

I'd only got into panties and a tight vest when he *did* come back.

"Well, that was the world's fastest shower." I turned to him as I unwrapped my hair from the towel.

He grinned shyly. "Yeah, well. I figured your uncle's home now, so I didn't want to spend too much time."

"He wouldn't mind you taking a long shower."

But he didn't answer, because his gaze had slowly travelled down my body, taking in my lack of clothes. And he *liked* what he saw.

"Roar..." I threw my towel on the desk and took a step towards him.

He finally met my gaze—and the silent communication we had right then only consisted of three words: *Need you now*.

I didn't know which one of us moved first, all I knew was we crashed together, bodies, lips, everywhere, and it was *frantic* and *fantastic*.

"Where'd you put the condoms?" he murmured against my lips once we'd moved to the bed. My panties were already off and his jeans were undone.

I fumbled for the bedside table drawer, but came up short.

He chuckled and leaned over to open it, plucking out one of the two packets left.

I didn't see him open it, because he bent down to kiss me. I didn't see him roll it on either, because that kiss was *so* good. But then his dick nudged against me and I spread my thighs wider, welcoming him.

It went a lot faster than our sexual escapade the day before, a lot wilder.

I grabbed onto the sheets as he thrust into me, right up against that legendary G-spot.

"Oh fuck!" I clutched at the duvet, the sheets, *him*, whatever I could get my hands on.

His lips descended on mine again, and we kissed sloppily through our shared pleasure. One of his hands gripped my thigh, hiking my leg up higher, while the other ran over my chest.

My nipples were hard pebbles through my thin vest and he pinched them.

I moaned loudly into his mouth, clutching at his neck now to keep myself right there against him.

Nice and slow was all well and good—but quick and rough sure weren't bad either! In fact, this right here and right now was so overwhelming, so over-consuming, that I could feel my orgasm build.

I'd never orgasmed so quickly before, nor from simply vaginal penetration. It was *wonderful*.

I closed my eyes and hugged him tighter through it, then let my arms drop listlessly down on the bed for that post-orgasmic bliss I hadn't felt in so long.

He still thrust into me, through his own orgasm, and I was *so* sensitive— but then he came, and he pulled all the way out, and he collapsed next to me on the bed.

We lay for a while in silence, simply letting our bodies calm down.

"Fuck." He rubbed his hands over his face. "Wow."

"Yeah," I agreed, staring dazedly up at the ceiling. Once I managed to string a sentence together, however, I turned my head to look at him. "Are we all right, Roar?"

He looked at me. "I don't know... aren't we?"

"I think we are." I frowned slightly. "I just

detected some awkwardness earlier. I don't want us to be awkward."

His chest rose and fell quickly. "What do you want us to be?"

I licked my lips, nervous all of a sudden when I hadn't been at all before. Apparently sex was no biggie, but a whole relationship chat was too much for me to handle. "I don't want us to be awkward, that's for sure." *Say it, Maria. Bloody say it!* "A couple? Boyfriend and girlfriend… that's what I want."

He blinked, then turned his head away. "Usually people don't want to be associated with me."

"So…?" I had no idea where he was going with that piece of information.

"If I hook up with someone, it's only for a night, you know. Or in secret, because no one can know they've shagged the school's loser."

I rolled onto my stomach and propped up so I could look down at him. "You're not a *loser*."

"I am." He gave me an embarrassed smile.

"People think you're dangerous. You're always getting into fights, and you show up with bruises and cuts on your face. People are scared of you."

Now I got his attention again—and his eyes were intense as they gazed into mine. "Why aren't you? Scared of me? I hurt you earlier. I could've done a lot

143

more than simply twist your wrist. So why aren't you afraid?"

"I startled you. It was my own fault."

He pressed his lips together. "Isn't that what women in abusive relationships always say?"

I laughed—I couldn't help it. "You're not an abuser, Roar. I startled you, and you're used to your stepfather beating the shit out of you, so of course you reacted the way you did. I could've been him. This was the first night you spent with me. I hope you'll get more comfortable as we spend more time together."

"You really want that?" There was something on his face and in his eyes... *hope*. Like he wanted this but didn't believe he *could* have it.

"Yeah." I kissed him, and hesitated a long time against his lips before I pulled back. But I only pulled back enough so I could look at him. "I want this. I want you." I stroked a hand through his hair, messing up his already ruffled wet locks. "You're not dangerous. Your stepfather is. You're just trying to make the most out of a shitty situation."

He wrapped an arm around my waist. "You'll make a good psychologist."

I chuckled. "You think so?"

"For how long have you known that's what you wanted to do?"

"Oh…" I didn't have to think long about it. "For about two weeks."

Now he seemed surprised. "Two *weeks*?"

"Yeah." I flicked my long, wet hair over my shoulder. "I've been thinking non-stop about what to do for months, and then I read about the psychology year course in the study handbook from the University in Trondheim… and I thought *I'd like to do this*. So I checked out the bachelor degree, and— yeah, I think it's the right thing for me."

"Well, you sure move quickly."

"I do, yeah, once I figure out what I want." I was pretty sure our words had a double meaning now. "So what do you say, Roar? Do you want to be my boyfriend?"

I knew he liked me—and pretty sure he wanted to pursue this. But pretty sure wasn't certain.

He chuckled. "I never pictured you like this."

"What do you mean?"

"Like this." He motioned to me, searching for words. "So straightforward, so open, so… *confident*."

I propped my head in the hand. "What did you picture me as then?"

He rolled his head a little against the sheets as he searched for words again. "Sweet, shy. I don't know. The kind of girl who never does anything wrong, does everything that's expected of her, someone shy and awkward about sex. Who'd never bring a lad home with her without anyone knowing. But you're not like that at all."

"Good. Because she sounds boring." I was perfectly aware of how my family saw me, as the quiet bookworm who preferred books over people. And to a certain extent that *was* me—but so was this.

I wasn't fond of throwing around the L-word, but I was quickly getting there with Roar. It was scary, but also exciting, and I'd never felt anything like this before.

It felt a little *dangerous*—like everyone said he was —and I couldn't get enough.

"She does," he agreed quietly, smiling softly.

"So is that a yes?"

Another smile split his lips, this one wider, happier. "Yes, Maria, I'd very much like to be your boyfriend."

I'd squeal, if I did such a thing, but settled for kissing him.

It was better anyway.

As his arms wrapped around me, pulling me down atop him, I knew we weren't going to get to school in time.

CHAPTER 15

*I*n the end, we both missed our first periods—but it was so worth it. We arrived at school before the bell rang for break, and we had the hallways all to ourselves for a few more minutes.

We spent those minutes wisely, snogging at the bottom of the stairs.

He pushed me up against the wall, and I cupped his face in my hands, all but devouring his lips. He was such a good kisser—kissing had never appealed to me like this with my ex.

"So I'm working tonight," he said when we pulled back for a break. "But we could go out for dinner after school? My treat this time."

"I'd like that." I wrapped my arms around his

neck. "And you're staying with me again tonight." I wasn't about to let him go home to that bastard of a stepfather he had. I wanted him with me, all safe and sound and preferably with no fresh bruises.

"Is that going to become a habit?" He teased my lip with his teeth.

"Maybe," I hedged. "Probably."

"Can't complain about that." He pushed up against me, flattening me against the wall. He was taller, wider, and a lot stronger than me—and having all that flush up against me turned me on like nothing else.

The bell rang.

"Dammit." I thumbed my head back, hitting the wall lightly. "See you at lunch?"

"You bet." He kissed me one more time, a soft, lingering kiss that neither one of us wanted to end.

"No fighting today." I took hold of his jumper, feigning sternness, but I *was* serious. "I don't care what people say about me. Let them talk. It doesn't matter. Just come join me at lunch and leave them to their sad gossip."

The sound of hundreds of feet came towards up, both from upstairs and the ground floor.

"No fights." Another kiss. "I promise."

We separated. He headed up the stairs while I ventured further ahead into the dance department.

I took my mobile up from my pocket as I walked.

So where would be best for me to corner Jasmin? Preferably alone. I don't want anyone else to know about this.

I sent that off to Iselin and went in search of my classroom. No one commented on my absence, simply because everyone had already left the classroom.

Nct to mention we had another teacher for second period, so not even that would be taken much notice of.

Upper secondary school was chill. Parents didn't have to write messages for their kids if they'd been gone from school for a day or an hour or a *minute*. Here we could come and go as we pleased—but it was obviously best to come and *stay*, as we wouldn't learn much otherwise.

My attendance record was pretty good though, so a few hours here and there wouldn't drag anything down for me. It wasn't like universities looked at that —all that mattered to them was the grades.

And when I were to apply for a job... well, they might look at it, but who would honestly put much trust in your attendance record from upper secondary school?

My phone vibrated and I plucked it up out of my pocket again.

> **Iselin:** *Well, Hedda's not in school today, so I reckon you can catch up with her whenever. Why don't you come over to our classroom when the bell rings for lunch? That way you can catch her before she goes off with someone.*

Lunch. I was going to meet Roar for lunch and I was loath to spend that half an hour with *Jasmin*. But whatever information she sat on was important—and I had to find out what it was.

I was about to send a text to Roar when I realised I didn't have his number—nor was he my friend on Facebook. I didn't even know his *last name*.

> **Me:** *What's Roar's surname?*

> **Iselin:** *You've shagged him and don't even know his name?*

> **Me:** *Stop judging me. Just tell me. I have to know.*

> **Iselin:** *OMG. It's Wangen. Roar Wangen. You should know this. You slag.*

Me: Not anymore I'm not!

Iselin: ??? You're over already? That was quick.

Me: NO! God. We're together. A couple. He's my boyfriend!

Iselin: You're kidding?!?!

Me: I wouldn't! Not about this. I'm so serious right now. We made it official this morning.

Iselin: Wow. Congrats! Wait… He's your BF, and yet you still don't know his last name?

Me: Oh, shut up. See if I tell you anything anymore.

I smiled to myself as I clicked into my Facebook app. Time to make Roar my friend on there, and then maybe… maybe something more.

But nothing came up when I searched for Roar Wangen. Not my Roar, anyway.

Maybe Iselin spelled it wrong?

I tried searching for Roar Vangen, but nothing there either.

"What the hell?" I muttered aloud, then stared up

ahead at the empty blackboard. *Who the hell doesn't have a Facebook nowadays?*

And that's exactly what I was going to ask Roar when we met up at the next fifteen-minute break.

"So who doesn't have a Facebook nowadays?" I planted myself in front of him, blocking his way out.

He glanced from me to my mobile, which I clutched in one hand.

"I don't."

"Why?" *Everyone* had Facebook.

He shrugged. "Why should I have it? It's not like I'd be very interactive on it."

"You will *now*. You've got me." I stepped closer to him so I could keep our conversation a little more private. "I was going to add you, only I couldn't find you. So you haven't got a Facebook, and I haven't even got your number."

He laughed. "I'll give you my number, Maria." He held his hand out expectantly and I put my phone in his palm.

He typed in his number and name, then handed it back.

"Thank you," I said.

"You're welcome." He snorted a laugh. "What did you need my number for anyway?"

"I reckon, at some point, I need to get a hold of you," I teased. "No, but for real. I have to talk to someone at lunch—if they'll talk to me, anyway. So until I get there, you can sit with Iselin?"

He raised an eyebrow sceptically.

"She's nice. And she doesn't bite."

"*Not* what I was worried about."

I tilted my head back slightly so I could look him in the eyes. "What were you worried about then?"

"We've got nothing at all in common. I don't think I've ever had a conversation with her."

I couldn't contain my laughter. "You're both slightly socially awkward. I think you would get along great." I patted his chest. "Okay? I have to figure some things out first, but I'll join you as soon as I can."

His eyes narrowed slightly. "What do you have to figure out? Are you all right?"

"I'm fine." Hopefully. What I didn't know couldn't hurt me and all that. If I was fine later depended on what Jasmin had to say. "I'll tell you all about it at dinner."

"I'll hold you to that."

I would hold *myself* to it. I'd just asked him to be my boyfriend, so I didn't want to start this relationship off with secrets. But I couldn't tell him anything before I had some answers myself, so this was it for now.

~

ONCE THE BELL rang for lunch, I hurried through the corridors towards Iselin's classroom. *And Roar's.*

People milled in the hallways, and I spotted both Iselin and Jakob in the throng heading towards the cafeteria.

I spotted Jasmin's long, dark, thick hair next to a locker. She stood alone, putting her books away, and I hurried over before she got surrounded by her gaggle of bimbo friends.

"Hey, Jasmin."

She stiffened, then slowly turned around to face me. Her face was carefully made up with make-up, eyebrows finely plucked and currently up in an arch that asked me what the hell I was doing talking to her.

"Can I talk to you?" I clutched my rucksack under one arm, nervous about what would come of this. "Somewhere more private?"

She rolled her eyes, but she headed into an empty classroom.

Once I was inside, she reached past me to close the door.

"If this is about that party—"

So she'd been expecting this, had she? "It is."

Her eyes narrowed at my interruption. "If you

think I wouldn't tell Hedda about you snogging her boyfriend, you're wrong—"

"This isn't about Jakob!" Why was everything about him? That had been sorted out. This was so much more important.

She crossed her arms over her chest. "What is it then?"

"Iselin said you were at that party, and since I don't remember much of it, I figured—"

"I'm not about to go into details of Jakob and you snogging. There were lips, tongues, maybe some groping, end of story."

"It's not about that either." I wrung my hands, all kinds of nervous now. She didn't make me feel any better with her attitude. "I don't actually remember hooking up with Jakob, but I've spoken with him. He didn't give me anything to drink. I was just wondering if you saw someone? Who gave something to me?"

She cocked her head curiously. "You don't remember anything?"

I shook my head. "Well, I remember arriving and sitting on the sofa drinking cider with Iselin... but apart from that, it's all blank until I woke up later that night."

"There was this guy who handed you a glass." She put her index finger to her lips thoughtfully.

"Maybe two? I don't know. You sat with him a little, at least."

"Who was he?" Why couldn't I bloody remember that night?

She blew out a breath and snapped her fingers. "M-something."

"Magnus?" *Please don't tell me my bloody ex has something to do with this.* We'd cut ties a long time ago. All we did lately was exchange a *hi* when we passed each other, but other than that we didn't talk.

"Umm, no." Jasmin still snapped her fingers. "But close. Marius?"

Marius? Who the hell was that?

"No, that's not right either. He's older, not in our school. He's Glenn's brother?"

My first thought was how in the hell did Jasmin know Glenn?

Then something cold slithered down my spine.

"*Marcus?*"

CHAPTER 16

"Yes! That's it." She seemed satisfied she'd remembered the name.

I, on the other hand, felt faint. "Did I—Did he—?"

She lowered her hands, expression softening. "I think he wanted something to happen, but you wandered off. Straight into Jakob's lap." She shrugged. "Then the two of you disappeared, and I don't have to be a genius to know what happened after that."

She pursed her lips. "So you don't even remember having sex with him? God, you had to be *so* pissed."

"Nothing happened," I said faintly, still stuck on Marcus.

What the hell had he been doing at that party? It had been a party for us still in school, not some older psychopath who'd almost *killed* Alex.

"Yeah, as if I believe that." Jasmin seemed oblivious to my horrification.

"It's true." I grabbed onto the desk behind me and leant against it. "I think he drugged me."

"Jakob?" She frowned. "I doubt he'd ever do something like that. The guy wears his heart on his sleeve."

"Not Jakob." I shook my head violently. "*Marcus.*"

"Oh. Well, if he did, he never touched you. Like I said, you walked away from him and straight over to Jakob. Well, okay, not *straight*, considering you weren't exactly steady on your feet, but you get my meaning."

I got her meaning all to well.

And I should be grateful it'd been Jakob I'd ended up with. Kind, troubled Jakob... if Marcus had got hold of me, I didn't even dare think about what he'd do to me.

The psycho had almost killed Alex because he was gay and dating his brother's best friend. What wouldn't he do to some poor drunk girl he'd drugged?

"What was he even doing there? He's a lot older

than us." Well, a lot was taking it a bit too far, but he was at least three years older.

Jasmin shrugged. "A lot of people were at that party."

"Did he give drinks to anyone else?" *Did he hurt anyone?*

"I don't know. I'm not his babysitter." Jasmin seemed annoyed now. "I had other things on my mind than look out for that idiot, okay?"

"So you're absolutely sure he didn't do anything to me?" Not that drugging me, if that was what he'd done, wasn't bad in itself. But it was the lesser of two evils. He could've just given me really strong drinks too, there didn't have to be any drugs involved.

I'd probably never get the truth though.

As long as that was it, I reckoned all was good.

Jasmin's expression softened again. "Yes, I am sure of that, Maria." She glanced around as if looking for other people, even knowing we were alone in the classroom. "I kept an eye on you. He seemed quite eager to get you drunk, so I kept an eye on you at all times. Until you disappeared with Jakob, anyway. Jakob's a decent guy—I figured I didn't need to look out for you anymore when you were with him."

"You just let me leave with your best friend's boyfriend?" I raised both eyebrows in wonder.

"It's none of my business what he does." She

flicked her long hair over one shoulder. "Hedda and he haven't exactly been doing so great lately. She was always going on about him, wondering if she should just break up with him. That he was the one who cheated surprised me, considering, but I'm glad they're over so I don't have to hear about him all the bloody time anymore."

"He didn't cheat though," I pointed out. "Not with me. We only slept in the same bed."

"Whatever happened, he grew some balls. Because he's not getting back with her. It's all good."

I didn't understand their friendship at all. "But she's miserable…"

"*He* made her miserable. She'll get over the breakup eventually and all will be good." She combed her fringe to the side with her fingers. "She wanted to sleep with him, he never wanted that. Hedda's wilder, she wants to party, be the centre of attention. He prefers to stay in the shadows. They're like night and day and they don't fit together. So yeah, I'm glad they're done. Now Hedda can find someone else, someone who's more of a match for her."

Huh.

Okay.

Jasmin looked straight at me. "And you can stop freaking out about that party. Marcus didn't do anything to you. And if he drugged you… well, nothing bad happened."

"Except I don't remember anything," I pointed out drily.

"You could've just had too much to drink," she pointed out too. "That causes black outs. I should know, I've had them plenty of times."

"Yeah, I know. Still… I don't trust him." I must've already been drunk if I'd even accepted drinks from him. I didn't want to get within a mile of Marcus.

"Didn't he get in trouble with the police or something last year?" Jasmin mused.

"Yeah. He bashed my brother's boyfriend in the head with an iron bar." And it wasn't last year, but the end of the year before. Still…

"He got in trouble for that, yeah?"

"Not as much trouble as he deserved." Not much trouble at all, really. Since Alex survived, and got no lasting damage, he got a pretty mild sentence. It was unfair—but it was the way it was. His mates stood up for him after all, so it was Andreas and Alex's words against the three of them.

Jasmin nodded, then turned to the door. "I'll be off then."

I followed her out of the classroom, more than ready be around people I knew and cared about.

She was going to the cafeteria too, and we walked

side by side, but we didn't say anything else to each other. As soon as we were inside, we parted ways.

I headed over to the table where Iselin and Roar sat in complete and utter silence. It was kind of funny, how they sat on opposites end of the table to each other, both immersed in their mobiles so they didn't have to look or speak to each other.

"Hey." I sat on the chair next to Roar, opposite Iselin.

She looked up at me in relief. "What did Jasmin say?"

"It's all good." I smiled at her, then at Roar, who shot me a wry glance. But he didn't pry into what we were talking about, just turned back to his mobile.

Now Iselin seemed relieved *for* me rather for me relieving the tension between her and Roar.

"Don't either of you have any lunch with you?" She glanced between Roar and me.

"Ahh, no. Didn't have time to make any."

When Iselin shook her head with a low, barely-there laugh, I knew she knew exactly why we hadn't had the time.

Because Roar's in her class and she knows he wasn't there for first period.

Oh well, I'd already told her we'd slept together, so it wasn't like it came as a shock to her.

"What are you doing after school?" Iselin asked then.

"We're going out to eat." I indicated Roar, who was still busy with his phone. After a quick glance over I saw he was scrolling through a news site.

Iselin nodded—at the exact same time as the bell rang.

"Already?" I sat up straight. "How long did I speak to Jasmin?"

"A while." Iselin stood and grabbed her rucksack from the floor. "See you later."

She walked off.

I put a hand on Roar's arm. "Hey."

"Hey." He finally put his mobile away and focused on me.

"We didn't even get to speak together."

He smiled crookedly. "That's okay. We'll speak after school."

Everyone around us moved slowly out of the cafeteria. We had to get a move on too if we wanted to get to our classes on time.

"See you later, then." I leaned over to kiss him— which seemed to surprise him. "Don't look at me like that."

"How am I looking at you?"

"All surprised." I stood up and stared down at

him. "Is it so wrong to kiss my boyfriend before we go our separate ways for class?"

He chuckled as he too stood. "No, I guess not. I just figured—well."

I had a feeling where this was going. "That I didn't want to kiss you in public?"

"Pretty much, yeah." He shrugged, like it wasn't a big deal, but it *was*.

"I don't mind kissing you in public. Or being seen with you. Or holding hands with you. Or snogging the shit out of you." I needed to get my point across. "I draw the line at sex in public, but as that's illegal, I figure that goes for most people."

He threw an arm around my shoulder as he burst out laughing, drawing me in to press a kiss to my temple. "You're so fucking great, Maria."

That pleased me endlessly to hear—and for that he got another kiss.

CHAPTER 17

I walked with Roar down to the gas station after we'd had dinner. During our meal, I'd told him about what Iselin had suspected last night, about what Jasmin had told me—but I hadn't given him Marcus' name.

He did have a reputation for fights, and considering he'd started a fight at school with some guy who'd only said stuff about me... I didn't want to think about what could happen if he found the guy who might have drugged me. Or at least got me so drunk I blacked out.

"You're staying with me tonight, yeah?" I asked as we stood outside the station.

"If you want me to."

"Oh, I do." I grabbed his hands in mine, squeezing.

"I have to go home and get a change of clothes though." He didn't seem like that was an exciting prospect.

"I can meet you down here at midnight, and we can go together," I offered.

He immediately shook his head. "No. No way. I don't want you anywhere near that miserable sod."

Maybe not, but I wanted to be there for him. "I can wait outside while you go in."

He found that somewhat more acceptable, because he nodded. "If you're absolutely sure."

"I am." I stroked his arm. "I'll see you again in seven hours, okay?"

He leaned down for a kiss and I sank eagerly into it, turning it into a deeper, longer kiss than he'd intended for it to be.

"Seven hours then." He squeezed me tight for a moment, then let me go and turned to head inside.

I stared after him, loathing that I had to wait seven hours to see him again. At the same time I got angry with myself, because I wasn't the type of girl who had to be with her boyfriend all the damn time.

Except I did want to be with him *all the time*.

I was turning into that girl.

I couldn't stand that. I often needed my privacy,

some time where no one were allowed to disrupt me. So I didn't want to become someone who was so dependant on her boyfriend she couldn't *breathe* without him.

"Maria?"

I whirled around at the voice—and came face to face with Jo. My cousin, and my sister's boyfriend. He was also *her* cousin, which had been weird at first, but I was used to it now.

"Oh, hey."

He stood next to his car, having just finished pumping gas. Which meant... if he'd just finished, he'd— "You saw that, huh?" My face flushed a little at the thought that he'd witnessed the way I'd kissed Roar.

"Kind of hard to miss." Speaking of, he seemed a little embarrassed himself.

Time to change the subject. "How's Christina?"

"She's at home, making dinner. You can come with me back home if you want?" He motioned to the passenger seat.

"Oh. Okay." It wasn't like I had anything better to do now Roar was at work for the next seven hours. And it had been a while since I'd seen my sister, so I reckoned I was due a visit.

I slid into the passenger seat and Jo got in front of the wheel.

"You been at work, or—?" I tried to get a conversation going, but I didn't quite know what to say to him. I was still embarrassed.

"Nah. Working later tonight." He started the car and drove away from the station.

That's what I'd already figured, seeing as he worked as a bartender, but work had been the only subject I could come up with at the top of my head.

It only took a few minutes to arrive at their flat, as they lived downtown. Jo parked at the kerb and I jumped out, waiting him for him to precede me over to the door to open it.

I followed him in, up the stairs, and then into their flat on the first floor.

"I'm home!" Jo called out. "And I brought someone with me."

"Who?" Christina stuck her head out of the kitchen. "Hey, sis!"

I waved. "Hey."

"Do you want dinner? I'm making tikka masala."

"No, that's okay. I already ate."

Jo headed into the kitchen to join Christina, and I followed after him.

My phone vibrated as I took a seat on a one of the three barstools at the counter, and I fished it out of my pocket to peer at it.

When I saw what it was, my eyes widened, and I

unlocked the screen to go into my Facebook app. But it said the same in there.

Jasmin had sent me a *friend request*.

Why the hell did Jasmin want to be my friend on Facebook?

"What's wrong?" Christina asked, clearly having taken my expression for something else.

"My life's getting too exciting." I put the mobile down, uncertain how to proceed now.

Christina laughed. "What's that supposed to mean?"

"There's this girl, at school. She's real popular, but rumour has it she's also a big slag. And now she's sent me a friend request."

Christina seemed confused. "How does she know who you are?"

I shrugged, then decided to be honest—or partially anyway. "We had a little chat today. I had to ask her about what happened at a party last weekend."

She laughed again. "Did you black out? I've had a few episodes like that. It's not fun. The hangover anxiety the next day is *brutal*."

"I know, right." Oh boy did I know. Though my anxiety might've been a bit worse than a regular hangover anxiety, considering what I'd been afraid of.

"So you went to a party, huh?" Christina turned to stir the sauce.

"It happens sometime. Like, once every leap year."

"Hah! So what else is new? We haven't spoken in a while."

"Umm…" I met Jo's eyes and he stared back with a serious expression. Since he already knew, it wouldn't be long till Christina found out anyway, so I might as well tell her. "I got a boyfriend."

Christina stiffened—then whirled around, excited. "What? Who? *When?*"

"His name's Roar. You don't know him." Or I hoped she didn't know him. "I met him Saturday, and now we're together."

Her eyebrows inched up her forehead. "That's four days ago."

I nodded, unsure what to say. People might think it was quick—and it *was*—but it felt so right for us.

"So you met him at that party you don't remember anything from?"

I shook my head. "Met him after. In the park. He helped me home."

"Were you that drunk?" Now she frowned, going into protective older sister mode.

"No, no," I hurried to say. "I just had a hard time walking in heels." Christina didn't need to know the other reason. I didn't want to make her worry for no reason—nothing had happened, after all. It was water under the bridge, and all that.

As for Marcus… if he *had* drugged me, there was nothing I could do about it. I'd probably never know the truth. And if he'd only supplied me with enough drinks to cause my blackout, then I deserved it for accepting all those drinks in the first place.

"And it was *really* cold outside," I added. "And I'd lost my jacket. Well, I'd lost it that night, but turns out Iselin had taken it home because she thought I'd left the party."

Christina laughed and shook her head, turning back to stir the sauce. "I've been there, so I know what it's like."

I reckoned she had. Christina liked to party—but at the same time she was also quite mature and protective. When she'd finished upper secondary school she'd stayed back for us—Andreas and I—because she didn't want to leave us after Dad died.

She seemed quite happy now though, so I didn't feel guilty for holding her back anymore. Jo made her happy, and that was the simple reason I'd overcome the initial weirdness of her dating my cousin way back when.

Jo kissed Christina on the cheek, muttered something I couldn't hear besides the word *shower*, and left the kitchen.

"So where's your boyfriend now?"

"At work."

"Where does he work?"

"At the gas station downtown. That's where I met Jo."

She turned to me again with a mock accusative glare. "So Jo found out before me? How rude!"

I laughed. "It was totally on accident, I swear."

She added the chicken to the sauce now and checked on the rice.

While she was busy, I turned to check my mobile again. Jasmin's friend request was still there.

I bit my lip, uncertain what it meant. Jasmin wasn't known for being the kindest person around. She was blunt—and she didn't hold her opinions back.

After our chat, I didn't get the feeling she particularly cared for me. So why in the world had she sent me a friend request?

What did it *mean*?

I'd never find out from ignoring it though.

I hovered my finger over my screen—then pressed down on *accept*.

Here it goes.

CHAPTER 18

" *M*aria!"

Jakob came hurrying up to me as I walked through the doors into the school the next morning.

"Hey." I smiled at him.

"I need to talk to you." He seemed anxious, and he shot Roar a pointed glance.

I swear Roar rolled his eyes. "See you at break," he told me, then took the stairs two steps at a time as he headed up to the first floor.

"What is it?" I asked Jakob, as it sounded serious. He *seemed* serious.

"Hedda keeps pestering me. Now she knows we didn't sleep together, she wants to get back together."

He stared resolutely at the floor. "I don't know what to do."

"How about telling her the truth?" I asked gently.

His shoulders sagged in defeat. "I think it's only way I'll get her off my back."

I could tell the prospect of telling her his biggest, darkest secret scared him like nothing else. "Hey, don't worry so much. What's the worst that can happen?" That might be a stupid question, as whatever could happen would feel bad for him.

"What if she tells everyone?" he muttered.

"Will your parents mind?"

He dithered a little. "I don't know. I think they'll mind me applying for a degree in teaching more, to be honest."

At least he wouldn't get disowned or thrown out or something else dramatic like that. It was stuff you only saw on TV anyway, stuff that didn't happen here in Norway. I hadn't heard about it happen here in Norway anyway.

Though, if they were as anal about his career as he said, maybe they'd do it for his *lesser* choice in education.

"I think she ought to know. That way she knows there can't be anything else between you." If she knew he was gay, there would be no point in her hassling him to get back together.

Or try to have sex with him, as being gay meant he wouldn't *ever* be interested in her assets.

"I know it's scary, though." Ben had gone through it too, though on a smaller scale. He'd been scared to death of telling our uncle. Though why he'd been scared, I had no idea, because Thomas had never expressed any views against homosexuality. He'd never expressed any negative views about *anything*. He was so easy-going, we could tell him whatever, and he'd take it with a smile.

Jakob glanced around subtly. "I don't want my friends to know. They're not the kind of lads to take it kindly. They're going to think I've been secretly trying to pull them all this time."

I narrowed my eyes. "That's the dumbest shit I've ever heard."

He shrugged awkwardly. "It's the way they are. They make fun of gay people. Like your friend Nik? He's so obviously gay. They made fun of him a lot last year."

My eyes narrowed into slits. "I don't like your friends." Nik was my second best friend other than Iselin. He was also Ben's best friend. And there was nothing funny about him—he was himself to the fullest, and I had utmost respect for him for that. "And if they can't accept you, they're not really your friends."

It was easy for me to say though, but not easy for him to take to heart. They *were* his friends. The only ones he had, and had had for years. It wasn't easy to mess with that.

The bell rang, ending our chat.

"Think about it, okay?" I patted his shoulder. "If the cons outweighs the pros of telling her the truth, don't do it. But you got to do something if you don't want her to keep pestering you."

He nodded quickly. "I know." He turned away. "I'll see you later."

I headed off to class, and I didn't see Jakob again until lunch. As per usual I sat on a table in the cafeteria, because it was still too cold to head outside. Jakob sat at a table on the other end of the room surrounded by his friends, but he didn't seem particularly happy.

"Careful, or I might get jealous."

I jumped in surprise as Roar murmured in my ear, then turned to watch him sit in the chair next to me. "You've got absolutely nothing to be jealous about. We're friends. I think." I glanced at him again.

Hedda was at their table too, but she didn't sit next to Jakob.

"Poor guy. He's got a lot on his mind."

"You want to share what exactly it is?"

"I can't. I promised to keep it a secret." And I'd

take that secret with me to the grave if I had to. I wasn't going to be the one to out him to anyone he didn't want to be outed to.

"All right then." He leant back on his chair and hooked his hands behind his neck. "I'm working again today."

"We doing the same as yesterday?"

"If you don't mind." The look he gave me told me clearly he'd much prefer it.

"I don't. At all." Which meant I'd head down to meet him at midnight, and we'd walk home to me and get into bed. It was a perfect ending to a day, to snuggle up in bed with him.

It meant I didn't get as much sleep as I was used to, as when I had school the day after, I was usually in bed by twelve… but it was so worth it.

"I think I'll spend some time with Iselin today," I said then, glancing around after her. It was weird that she hadn't joined me in the cafeteria yet. "I feel like I've been ignoring her a little for the past few days."

He only nodded silently.

It made me feel a bit melancholy, because he didn't have any friends. No one to spend his time with outside of school and work. He only had me— or his abusive stepfather, and if I had any say in the

177

matter he wouldn't be heading back there to sleep anytime soon.

I tugged on his elbow and when he untangled his hands from around his neck, I took his in mine and tangled our fingers together. "You all right?"

He'd had a run-in with his stepfather last night, when we'd stopped by there so he could pick up some clothes. The arsehole hadn't hit him again—he still had the shiner under his eye from last time, after all—but he'd been downright nasty.

I hadn't witnessed it, because as we'd agreed, I'd waited outside.

Still, I'd been able to tell he'd been upset when he'd finally come out—and on our way home I'd managed to drag it out of him.

"So my sister and her boyfriend know about us now." I'd forgot to tell him that, what with his stepfather and all last night. "Jo saw us at the gas station when you went to work. He saw us kiss."

"Were they okay with it?" He eyed me curiously.

"Sure. Why shouldn't they be?" I tilted my head slightly to the side to stare back at him. "I think I should tell my uncle soon, too."

"Yeah, considering I've practically lived there for the past two days, I think you should." He chuckled. "It'll be real awkward the day I *do* meet him and he doesn't have a clue who I am."

"I'm going to tell him. Maybe this weekend? I don't know. Alex and Leo are coming home, like usual. I'm not sure I want to break something like this around the dinner table with them all." I shuddered at the thought of all their eyes on me—not to mention what Ben would have to say about the matter. "If Ben meets you, he'll probably start to hit on you."

That earned me a startled laugh out of him. "Trust me, you've got nothing to worry about there."

"Oh, you don't know Ben. He's really charming." He'd managed to hold onto Tarjei for four years, for some reason way beyond me, and he needed proper skills for that. Considering what I'd heard about Tarjei—that he shagged whoever, whenever, whatever... it was a wonder he kept coming back to Ben.

But their weird relationship wasn't something I wanted to dwell on. It was none of my business.

Ben could live his life the way he wanted, shag whoever he wanted—and I could do the very same.

But I was sticking to only one guy.

The best guy.

In the end, Iselin didn't show up at lunch, so I spent the entire half hour talking with Roar. We went out to eat again after school, and after I walked with him down to the gas station.

"See you at midnight." I leaned up for a kiss, which he gladly gave me.

"I can manage the walk back to you on my own," he said. "So you don't have to come all the way down here." He slid his arms around me, drawing me in close.

"But I want to." Losing a little sleep didn't matter. Tomorrow was Friday anyway, which meant I didn't have school until third period. It was worse for him, who had to be there by the regular eight thirty. "See you."

After another lingering kiss, I pulled away.

My phone vibrated in my pocket and I took it up to check what was going on as I walked. It was a message from Jakob, and I unlocked my screen to check what he'd written.

Jakob: So I did it. I told her.

Me: How did she take it?

Jakob: Okay, I think? She wasn't happy though. But I hope she understands now.

Me: That's good! Great for you, Jakob. One more person

who knows the truth.

Jakob: Heh, yeah. Maybe some day, once school's over, I'll tell my friends too.

Me: Why when school's over?

Jakob: Because that's when we go our separate ways. I won't have to worry about how they react then, because we're all heading off in different directions anyway.

Me: You know what, you're coming over to my place this weekend. Alex is coming home, and I think you two should meet.

Jakob: Alex? Your brother?

Me: No, my brother's boyfriend. Andreas is in the army. I have no idea when he's coming home next time. But you should totally meet him too.

Jakob: All right. As long as you're not trying to set me up with anyone.

Me: LOL. You wish. Alex is with my brother after all. And I wouldn't ever. I'm keeping you away from Ben!

Jakob: Maybe I should.

Me: Should what? Get with Ben???

Jakob: Yeah. I don't know. Maybe I should get laid? Get it over and done with.

I stared down at my phone, somewhat taken aback to learn he was a virgin. I shouldn't be surprised though, considering he'd told me he'd never given in to Hedda's advances.

Trust me, Jakob, you want your first time to be special. Not with someone you don't even know.

My first time had been with my ex, and it had been special at the time. Not so much now when I thought about it, but it was what it was.

And nothing bad about Ben—I loved the lad to bits, but he got on my nerves at times, and he was a total slag. Jakob was quickly becoming a good friend and I didn't want him to end up in bed with my *cousin*—or be screwed over by him. Because Ben didn't do anything but oneoffs, unless it was Tarjei. He always ended up back with Tarjei.

If those two didn't figure their shit out soon...

Jakob: Yeah, you're right. I'm going to wait until university. That way I won't have to worry about my friends or parents.

I felt sorry for him. He had so much to take into consideration, simply because he was afraid to come out. And he apparently had good reason to be afraid, which sucked.

Jakob: I did apply for schools today. Applied in Trondheim and Volda, the closest ones, but also places further away. I hope to get into one of the first two though. I want freedom, but I don't want to be too far from home.

I got that one. It was the same thought process I had. I wanted to be able to go home for a weekend, without too long a travel that would eat into time spent with my family.

Me: I have to apply too.It completely skipped my mind the applications are open. Need to figure out what Roar wants to do though.

Jakob: You're that serious? You want to go to school together?

Me: I don't know. I mean, if we're together by fall I want to at least be in the same town as him. Maybe we can room together. Maybe the three of us could room together if we end up in Trondheim, huh? That would be neat. And save us all on rent, because it's expensive up there!

Jakob: Rooming together sounds like a good idea! What about Iselin? Aren't you going to room with her?

Me: No, Iselin's heading down south. She wants to be a veterinarian—and with her perfect grades, she'll definitely get in. So she'll be in Oslo for at least three years.

This fall would be the very first time I'd be without my best friend. We'd been together so long it was unreal to even think about the fact we would be so far apart.

I was slowly making new friends—Roar and Jakob—but none could eve replace Iselin. I'd miss her so much once school was over and we went out separate ways.

So that was why I headed to her house. It was time for some best friend bonding.

CHAPTER 19

I spent the entire evening with Iselin—to the point I had to run out her door right before midnight if I wanted to be downtown in time for Roar to get off work.

I didn't make it.

In the end, I was ten minutes late.

Roar was outside, the doors were closed and the gas station dark. But he wasn't alone. In front of him stood another figure, with his back to me.

I saw him slip something to Roar.

Roar slipped something back.

My heart started beating quicker. I had no idea what was going on, it could simply be something trivial as Roar buying something for a friend before he closed the shop.

But Roar has no friends.

Iselin's warning, about the rumour she'd heard Roar was on drugs… it was forefront on my mind.

"Roar!" I called out, alerting them to my presence.

He looked up at me, eyes widening a little.

The person in front of him turned half-way—and I froze.

It wasn't just anyone Roar was talking to—it was bloody *Marcus*. The psycho arsehole who almost killed Alex, who got me drunk and possibly drugged me.

And he'd just slipped something to Roar…

Anger made me brave, and I stalked towards them.

"What are you doing here?" I demanded of Marcus.

He regarded me lazily. "I think the better question is why are *you* here. Go home little girl." He made a *shooing* motion, as if I was an annoying little brat.

I clenched my hands. "What did you do to me?"

His eyebrows drew together.

"On Saturday! What did you *do* to me?" I stepped closer to him, ignoring Roar entirely for now. "Did you only get me drunk or did you drug me too?"

"What?" This was Roar and he now glanced from me to Marcus and back at me again.

Marcus' frown deepened. "What the hell?"

"⁻ know you were there. I know you gave me drinks." My hands shook from nerves and adrenaline and anger. "Do you get off on drugging girls? Is that the only way you ever get anything?"

His lips pressed together into a thin line. "I warn you, Maria—"

"You *warn* me? Lucky me. You didn't warn Alex when you hit him in the head with an iron bar." Besides the fact that Alex could've *died*, the whole incident had messed them both up a lot.

I couldn't ever forgive this arsehole for that.

If he'd done something to me... well, then I'd march straight up to the police station and press charges. With a second felony, he surely wouldn't get off as lightly this time around. Not even with his brilliant attorney parents.

Marcus sneered now.

"Drugging someone is illegal. If I go press charges right now—"

"You can't without evidence!" His face turned slightly red.

"You already have one incident on your criminal record. You think they're going to let this go, even if I've got no evidence? It'll be in your *file*." I didn't know where this bravery came from, this need to confront him. It felt good to do it, but also terrifying.

"I *didn't* drug you, you mad cunt!" He took a step

back. "Yes, I gave you drinks, but you were already pretty pissed. I didn't do *shit* to you."

I believed him, because my threat about pressing charges clearly had him in a bit of a panic.

"You better not have." Jasmin's recollection of events helped a lot with my believing him too. She'd sworn he hadn't done anything to me, after all.

Marcus gave me a disgusted look, then strolled off with a shake of the head.

I turned slowly to face Roar, who stood still and silent behind me.

"What did he give you?"

"Give me?" He seemed honestly confused.

I licked my lips. "You exchanged something. What was it? Marcus isn't in the business of trading lollipops, that's for sure." I didn't want to demand answers from him, I wasn't the type of girl who intruded like this... but Marcus was dangerous and whatever dealings Roar had with him couldn't be good.

Roar looked away and bowed his head. "Pills," he muttered. "He gave me some pills. I paid for them."

My heart sank. "What kind of pills? Are you on drugs?"

Had the rumours been right for a change?

Please tell me they're not right.

"They're to keep me awake," he admitted in a low

voice. but then he squared his shoulders and straightened up to look straight at me. "I take them sometimes to stay awake, when I can't go home, when I'm at work, and then got school in the morning. Because without them I'd be a bloody zombie."

"What kind of drugs is it?" I had no particular knowledge about drugs. I didn't know which one could keep a person awake. Was it cocaine? Meth? Ecstasy?

"It's not a narcotic, if that's what you think." He drew a small plastic bag out of his pocket to show me the pills inside it. "They're used for treating narcolepsy. To keep those who suffer from it awake. It works on people without narcolepsy too, though, and it keeps me focused at school after nights where I've had no sleep."

The fight went out of me at his words.

Was it really so bad for him he had to stay out for entire nights? "Roar…"

"It is what it is." But he looked away, seemingly unable to look at me. His hand clenched around the small plastic bag. "I don't take them because I *want* to. I do it because I have to. Sometimes I have no other choice."

Bloody hell.

"Let's go home, Roar." I reached out to him and grabbed his free hand. "Come on." I tugged and he came, and we walked side by side away from the gas station. "Whenever you can't go home, even if it's every night, come to *me*. There's always room for you in my bed. It's a safe place, where no one's ever going to hurt you."

He stared down at the ground as we walked. "Okay." But his voice sounded flat.

"What is it?" He'd slept at my place for two nights. Surely he wouldn't need any of those pills *now*?

He bit down on his lip. "Marcus... did he really drug you?"

Is that it? I sighed. "I don't know. All I know is I don't remember shit from that night. It could've just been the alcohol, because people get blackouts from drinking all the time... but Iselin put the idea into my head and it scared me. When Jasmin told me Marcus gave me drinks, I instantly though— well, he's fucking *mental*. He could've *killed* Alex."

"I know he's not right, that he's a bad person to be around. But he's *the* person if you need something you can't obtain legally, you know?"

"Come sleep with me and you won't have to commit felonies to stay awake." I leaned my head against his shoulder.

"Sleep *with* you?" A wry grin spread slowly on his lips.

"Oh, you know what I mean!" I slapped his chest playfully. "But, yes, that too."

I hooked my arm around his elbow and we walked for a while in silence.

"Stay with me Roar, and you won't ever have to deal with your arsehole of a stepfather."

"I'd still have to go back there once in a while."

"But you don't have to stay there." Thomas wouldn't mind Roar staying at the house. He liked a full house, considering even Leo came back every weekend with Alex now.

"We'll see," was all he said, with an embarrassed smile.

We were at the house now. Thomas' car was in the driveway—and so was Leo's.

They'd arrived already? It was only Thursday. Maybe they had Friday off school.

"Full house tonight," I said, "so we better be quiet."

I let us in and we walked silently over the floor to the stairs. They creaked slightly on the first few steps, but not loud enough to be heard upstairs.

I went first, and Roar followed after me.

The light was on, so I saw where I was going. When I was only a couple steps from the top, Thomas' bedroom door opened—

And Leo came out.

CHAPTER 20

I blinked at him.

He stared at me.

"Leo?"

I glanced at the door behind him. Thomas' bedroom door. Which Leo was coming out of in the middle of the night—

"Oh."

Roar shuffled behind me, drawing Leo's attention away from me.

"Ahh—" I cast a quick glance over my shoulder at Roar, then faced Leo again. "I don't tell your secret and you don't tell mine?" I even thrust my hand out towards him.

"Uhh." But he took my hand and we shook on it. "All right then."

I pressed my lips together, gaze going from Leo to Thomas' bedroom door. "So that's what it's like, huh?" I hadn't even had a tiny flicker of suspicion of their relationship being anything but friendly.

"Yeah." Leo seemed faintly embarrassed.

"Huh." When had it happened? What the *hell*? "Okay then. Good night." I turned to Roar, who stood with his head bowed. Didn't he want to draw attention to himself? Had he turned suddenly shy? Or did he want to hide the bruise still adorning his eye?

We headed past Leo and down the hall into my bedroom.

Once the door was shut, I leant back against it with a sigh. "I had *not* expected *that*."

Roar sat on the bed. "So your uncle's gay?"

I tilted my head from side to side thoughtfully. "I don't know. Seems that way?" Or he could be bi. I'd never actually seen Thomas with anyone before. He'd never introduced a special someone to the family. He'd always been alone.

"So who was that guy?" Roar looked at me steadily.

"That was Leo. Alex's brother."

"Alex, your brother's boyfriend?"

I nodded.

"So your brother's boyfriend's brother is shagging your uncle?" He tried to wrap his head around the relations.

"It seems so, yeah."

Why had I never noticed them? Sure, Leo'd been around ever since Christmas, and they always seemed to get along great, but I'd never suspected anything else to be going on between them.

"Does it bother you?" he asked, eyes narrowing a little as he studied me.

"No." Of course it didn't. "I just didn't know. I didn't notice anything off—or on in this situation, I suppose—between them."

"Come here." Roar motioned me over.

I went.

He put his hands on my hips, drew me in close, and I straddled his thighs.

"As long as Thomas is happy, *I'm* happy." I hooked my arms around his neck. "He deserves someone special in his life. He's always been alone. Taking care of Ben, of us. We're all leaving soon now, and he'll be all on his own. If he's got someone, if he's got Leo, that's very good."

Roar fell back on the bed—and he brought me with him.

I braced my arms on either side of his head and leaned down to kiss him.

He cupped my arse, hands running over, fingers teasing my crotch.

"We don't have anymore condoms," I muttered against his lips. We'd used the three I'd stolen from Ben, and I didn't dare go down and steal more from him.

"I bought a pack before I closed the gas station." Roar reached into his pocket and, yes indeed, he pulled out a pack of standard condoms.

I laughed quietly and nipped at his lip. "Good thinking."

It was late, we had another day of school in the morning—but sex was too tempting to pass up.

When he had me spread on the bed, thighs parted, and he was eating me out... it was so good I had a hard time keeping quiet. Knowing Leo couldn't be asleep yet, I did manage to keep my mouth shut, but it was damn difficult to do.

Roar worked his tongue expertly—and I was *this* close to coming when he pulled back.

I opened my eyes to protest, but once I saw him put a condom on, I kept quiet. I only spread my legs wider, accommodating him in-between them, and arched my back as he sank into me.

It was so good and I didn't know what to do with myself until he flipped us around and I suddenly had to do all the work.

His hands cupped my tits—not that there were much to cup—while I rose and fell on him.

My thighs weren't used to this kind of activity at all, and they burned, but it felt too good to stop.

His dick rubbed right up against my G-spot in this position and I was quickly coming undone.

He wasn't far behind me.

After, I snuggled up against his side and he wrapped an arm around me.

We fell asleep like that without another word to each other.

ROAR LEFT EARLY NEXT MORNING, as school started eight thirty as usual for him. I lay in bed for another hour before I got up.

I had breakfast with Thomas and Leo, which was awkward. I knew about them, but Thomas didn't know I knew, so Leo and I kept glancing at each other.

I headed to school early so I could catch up with Roar during break.

As soon as I entered the school yard, Jasmin came striding towards me.

"Is it true?" she demanded.

I frowned in confusion. "What?"

"About Jakob. Is he gay?"

I stopped dead. "Where'd you hear that?"

"Hedda's told everyone." Jasmin shrugged.

"She's *what*?" That *bitch*. "Where's Jakob?"

Jasmin shrugged again. "He left. After first period."

Anger bubbled up inside me, replacing the shock of what Hedda had done. She'd done what Jakob had feared worst. "Where's Hedda?"

Jasmin motioned across the school yard, where Hedda stood in a circle with Jakob's male friends.

I strode towards them, ignoring the guys, and focusing fully on Hedda. She didn't see me coming.

"How dare you do that to him?" I asked.

She turned, face set in a grim grimace. "He got what he deserved."

She wasn't even *repentant*. "You're such a fucking bitch. No wonder he doesn't want to be with you."

Her lips thinned and whitened. "You're the one who messed us up in the first place."

I shook my head even before she finished speaking. "Oh, I'm not. But I advised him to tell you the truth. I thought you were a decent person who would keep shut about it. But no... you spread it around out of *spite*."

This time around I was the one who hit *her*.

Hedda gasped in surprise, hand going to her

cheek, but then she dropped her bag and jumped on me.

We fell to the ground with a loud *thud*, my back taking the brunt of it. But I wasn't going to let her claw at my face and I fought her with all I had.

She screamed something, but I didn't catch it, because I was too busy fighting off her slaps. Her nails were long and sharp and they'd do real damage if I let them anywhere near my face.

We rolled on the ground. There were sounds above us, but I couldn't make out words. All that mattered was to get one over Hedda—and I did, because I was on top, pinning her down—

Except she managed to buck me off her, and now she was on top of *me*, and she raised her hand—

And a hand locked around her wrist, so she couldn't budge. She turned her head, outraged, and I took my chance and bucked her off me.

"Let go of me!" Hedda tried to rip her hand out of the iron grip, but the hand holding hers didn't budge.

I looked up—and saw it was Roar who'd stopped her from hitting me.

I pushed up on my knees, then onto my feet, and brushed dirt off my clothes.

Hedda still struggled to get her hand out of Roar's grip, and when he suddenly released her without warning, she fell down on her hands and knees.

He strolled over to me without another look down at her.

"You all right?"

I nodded quickly, a bit too shaken up to speak.

He threw an arm around my shoulder and steered me away from Hedda, who got to her feet now as well.

"You've hooked up with him now?" Someone shouted, and when I looked over my shoulder, I saw it was my ex—Magnus. "You should've stuck to Jakob, made sure he wasn't such a poof. You'll only get in trouble with *that one*." He spat the last two words out.

The weight of Roar's arm left my shoulder, and in the next second his fist had connected with Magnus' face.

I stood back silently, shaky from the adrenaline my fight with Hedda had brought on, and more than happy to let Roar beat some sense into Magnus' idiot head.

Jakob's friends gathered around the two, shouting and egging the fight on.

Hedda stood outside the ring, clutching her wrist.

I gave her a hard stare, daring her to try anything.

She glared back, but stayed where she was.

"Maria!" Iselin was at my side now. "Are you all right?"

"I'm fine." I turned back to the circle of lads. I couldn't see Roar—I didn't know if he was winning or losing. All I could hear were the yells and egging of all the other blokes gathered around.

Maybe not completely fine.

My back ached, from where it had taken the brunt of my fall earlier. Not to mention taking both my own body weight *and* Hedda's.

Someone had stepped in to break up the fight— and Roar pushed his way past all the arseholes gathered around and stalked over to me.

He had a split lip, but seemed otherwise fine.

Iselin looked at him too, but with some trepidation.

"Want to skip school today?" I took his hand and squeezed.

He only nodded.

I looked at Iselin, who still stared at Roar. "You going to class? Or do you want to come with us?"

"Skip school?" She glanced back at the double doors, biting her lip. "I've never skipped school before."

"There's a first time for anything." It wasn't like her grades would suffer from one day off.

All the lads gathered around Magnus broke up as

the bell rang. Magnus seemed worse for wear than Roar—he also had a split lip, but he was also swollen and red over his cheekbone and side of the eye.

Good riddance.

Last year I'd thought Magnus hung the moon, before I started seeing him anyway, and during the start of our relationship. I'd eventually come to realise what a twat he was—sadly I'd already started to put out for him before it got to that point.

Hedda was at his side, and she glared at me.

The fucking bitch.

"Does anyone know where Jakob lives?" I looked between Roar and Iselin, who both shook their heads. "I have to go see him. *We* have to." It seemed his friends had abandoned him once Hedda spread the truth around—and whatever other vile lies she'd spun with it.

I took my phone up and quickly typed in a message to him.

Where are you? I just came to school and heard what happened. I'm so sorry! Roar and I are skipping school. Lets meet.

Next I looked back up at Iselin. "You coming with us or what?"

Her teeth sank further into her bottom lip.

"You don't have to," I said softly, hating to see her struggle with what was right and wrong.

"I think Jakob needs someone more right now than I need to be here." But she cast a hesitant look back at the doors.

My phone vibrated and I quickly unlocked the screen to see what Jakob had answered.

Jakob: *I'm at the park. You can meet me here?*

Me: *We can go to BK? Get something warm to eat and just hang out? Iselin's coming too.*

Jakob: *Okay…*

Me: *Don't worry, Jakob. We're here for you.*

"He's at the park." I turned away from the school. "Shall we go?"

Roar, who hadn't pulled his hand out of mine, turned with me.

Iselin nodded, face set, and came up on my other side. "Yeah, lets."

So we left the school behind and headed downtown.

CHAPTER 21

*J*akob sat on a bench, with his elbows on his knees and head in his hands. He seemed defeated and sad and lost.

"Hey, Jakob." I let go of Roar's hand, which I'd held onto ever since we left the school, to put mine on Jakob's shoulder.

He slowly let his hands drop, but he didn't look up. "She told *everyone.*"

"I know." I sat down next to him and glanced up at Roar and Iselin, who hung back a little. Neither of them knew Jakob, after all. "Come on, lets head to BK, stuff our faces, talk, and have fun."

He glanced at me—then at them.

"That's what friends are for." I stood up again and patted his shoulder.

He rose with a defeated sigh. "I'm not sure what to do now."

"You be proud of who you are." There was nothing else for it. He couldn't skip school forever, or avoid everyone *at* school forever. And I wasn't going to let him go around and be ashamed. "The truth's out there. Own up to it."

He scratched awkwardly at his neck. "Easy for you to say. You're straight."

"But I've got a gay cousin, a gay best friend, and a bi brother," I pointed out. "Plus I know lots of other people who aren't straight. There's nothing wrong being attracted to someone of the same gender."

I'd watched Ben struggle with telling Thomas, whereas Andreas had never told anyone at all—he'd simply brought Alex home, and he'd never left. And now Leo was part of our family too, somehow, besides simply being Alex's brother.

"I'm straight," Roar shot in, looking straight at Jakob with a serious expression. "But you don't see me go around outing people or mocking them for who they like to sleep with. What people do in the bedroom is frankly none of my business."

Iselin licked her lips, then hitched a thumb Roar's way. "What he said."

I hooked my arm around Jakob's elbow. "See?

You're not all alone. We're here. We don't tell secrets, or spread rumours, or call anyone names. Except Hedda, but after what she did, she deserves to be called a bitch."

That brought a small smile out on Jakob's face.

"So you up for Burger King?" I asked him.

"Yeah, okay."

I let go of his arm and fell into step besides Roar. He had his hands buried in his leather jacket now, but that was okay. I wasn't *that* fond of public displays of affection—holding hands all the way over here had been more than enough PDA for me for one day.

We left the park behind and headed down to the main part of town.

Roar's head turned to watch a man amble up the pavement across the street. He lugged three bags form the liquor store with him.

"My stepfather," Roar murmured in a low voice so only I would hear.

I looked closer at the man. He seemed dishevelled, like he hadn't showered in days or cut his hair in months. He wore baggy clothes, but he was quite tall and bulky, and not even the baggy clothes could hide that.

"He used to be into body-building," Roar explained. "So he's all buffed up. Now he's all about drinking, but he's still so fucking strong. I can't take him."

I moved my focus over to Roar. He was tall too, but not near the man across the street from us. And he was lanky. He had muscles, but he was more toned, not all bulked up like his arsehole of a stepfather.

"I'm sorry, Roar." But he wasn't alone anymore. He had me, and now he had Iselin and Jakob too.

"It's not your fault." He bumped me playfully. "Besides, if I could've taken him, I don't think I would've stopped hitting until he was dead." He looked over his shoulder, watching his stepfather amble up towards home.

Yeah, maybe it is a good thing. Because if Roar had hit his stepfather until he died, he certainly wouldn't be walking besides me now.

I wanted him beside me.

We fit so nicely together.

Iselin and Jakob had stopped, waiting for us to catch up with them. They hadn't heard what we'd been talking about, which was good.

It had been private—and they didn't need to know Roar harboured such deep-seated loathing for his stepfather to the point he knew he could kill him if he snapped.

～

FOUR TRAYS of food filled the table and all four of us dug in. The chips were warm and crisp and salty, and with a healthy dose of ketchup on them, it was heaven.

Jakob still seemed down, but I hadn't expected any different. His life had just been turned tits up, after all. He nibbled on his hamburger, a distant look on his face.

"Do your parents know yet?" I asked, as he'd told me he'd been worried about them. Not so much the gay thing, but the school thing. Still...

He shook his head. "I haven't been home since I left for school. They're at work anyway, it's not like they're going to hear about it anytime soon unless Hedda personally shows up at my house to tell them." He grimaced, and it seemed like he wouldn't put that past her at this point.

"Maria hit her," Roar said, hitching a thumb at me.

"What?" Jakob's eyes widened.

I gave Roar a *look*. "Thanks for that." When he only grinned and took a bite of his burger, I turned back to Jakob. "But, yeah, I did. I found out from Jasmin. She asked me if it was true. Then I found Hedda—and I hit her. She deserved it."

A startled laugh left Jakob and he put his burger down on his tray. "You *didn't*."

"She totally did," Iselin shot in. "It was epic."

"I've never hit anyone before," I mused. "Except that time she hit *me* and I hit back. But that was more self-defence than anything."

"Did you like it?" Jakob asked, a wry smile slowly spreading on his lips.

"Kinda did, yeah."

Roar choked down a chuckle next to me.

"Right now I wish *I* could hit her." Jakob folded his hands and rocked forward a little."

"You could," I offered, "but I reckon you'd probably get in trouble. It's a bit double standard. Women can hit a man without getting in trouble with the law, but as soon as a man hits a woman, he's an abuser. Many times that's true—but some women deserve to be hit."

"Amen to that." He lifted his cardboard box full of Cola and tilted it against my milkshake.

"Second that." Iselin joined with her Sprite.

Roar only shook his head, but he smiled.

We dug back into our food, but Jakob didn't seem to be in better spirits. In fact, he seemed downright depressed.

"Whatever happens at school, we're here for you," I said, trying to console him. "Whatever they say or do, come hang out with us. We're not judging."

He managed a small smile around his straw. "I appreciate that."

I twiddled with my own straw. "So… Are you going to tell your parents?" I was a bit worried about how that would go for him. But surely they couldn't be as nasty as Hedda?

To think that Jakob had thought their chat to go well, only for her to turn around and do something so vindictive…

"I reckon I have to. They'll find out eventually anyway." He hitched one shoulder. "It's better to break the news of my sexuality than what I've applied to school for, anyway."

Iselin and Roar shot him wry looks at that.

"What have you applied for?" Iselin asked curiously.

"I want to be a teacher." He gave her a small, sad smile. "They don't think that's a good career choice. Anything that isn't lawyer or engineer or a doctor isn't a good career choice."

Iselin's eyebrows drew together into a frown. "That sucks."

"Yeah." He sighed and looked down at his tray.

"So they're not going to throw you out for being gay then?"

"I don't think so."

"If they *do*," I shot in, "we've got a room available at my house you can stay in."

Now Iselin shot *me* a wry look. "You do? Aren't all rooms taken?"

"Christina's is available."

"But doesn't Leo have that when he's around?" she asked, frowning. She knew everything about what went on in my house, though she'd never met neither Leo nor Alex.

"Uhh…" Well, shit. That was supposed to be a secret, wasn't it? "Not… really." I wanted to have the offer out there, in case of worst case scenario for Jakob, but that meant I had to *tell* that secret. "Swear you won't tell anyone?"

Iselin blinked. "Please don't tell me he's shagging Ben."

A laugh escaped at that. Iselin knew just how much of a slag Ben could be. "No, he's not. But you're not that far off, actually. But really, you can't tell *anyone*."

"I won't." Iselin made a cross over her heart.

"Leo and Thomas," was all I said as I hooked my middle finger over my index finger, "they're *tight*."

"What? Really?" Iselin leant forwards, voice falling a little. "I didn't know your uncle was gay."

I shrugged. "I don't know what he is. As long as

he's happy, I'm happy. If anyone deserves to be happy, it's Thomas. After everything he's done for us during all these years… But this is *top secret*. I think I'm the only one who knows."

"Secret relationship, huh?" Iselin got a dreamy look on her face. "That's romantic."

Both Jakob and I laughed, while Roar raised an eyebrow.

"What do you know about romance?" I asked through my laughter. "You're not romantic *at all*."

"I can still appreciate the romance of others." Iselin made a mock-indignant grimace, before a giggle escaped.

"We're a right bunch, aren't we?" I looked around at the three of them. "But I think we fit together anyway." Roar and Jakob hadn't said much to each other, but I had a feeling they'd get there eventually.

That we'd all get there.

For so long it had only been Iselin and me. Best friends since forever. Then I'd started to get to know Roar and Jakob at the same time, and now here we were. A rag-tag group of loners.

Well, except Jakob as he'd been a part of the popular crowd, but now he was with us.

He'd fit in better with us, anyway.

CHAPTER 22

*R*oar pulled double shifts at the gas station both Saturday and Sunday, so he didn't get to meet any of my family—or Leo.

First on Monday, after school—when he actually had a day off because of changing the schedule around for the week—did he get to meet Thomas.

Roar walked home with me right after school.

We'd left with Iselin and Jakob, and separated to each our houses on the way. It had been a long, awkward day—with Jakob trying to avoid all of his friends.

Former friends by now, perhaps.

Hedda had been cuddled up with Magnus—and I wished her *good luck* with that. As long as she left

Jakob alone, as long as she didn't make him anymore miserable, I was happy.

Roar hadn't been home in days, which meant he hadn't run into his stepfather at all. His black eye was faded now, to the point it passed as shadows, hard to notice unless someone looked *real* close.

"Hello!" I called once I was in the door, after seeing Thomas' car in the driveway.

"In the kitchen," he replied, voice lower and softer than mine.

I went over to the doorway. "I brought someone home with me," I said.

Thomas turned to look at me "Are you asking my permission?"

"Oh, no, it's just so you know, is all. It's someone I want you to meet."

"Someone special?" he asked.

"Yes, someone very special." I turned around to look at where Roar stood out in the hall, somewhat nervous.

I motioned for him to come closer.

He had to come close enough so Thomas could seem him from the kitchen.

"Uncle, this is Roar, my boyfriend."

Thomas stared at Roar—Roar stared back.

"Hi. Nice to meet you." Roar's voice was lower than normal.

He's still nervous.

Thomas dried his hands on a cloth and came across the kitchen floor. He thrust his hand out towards Roar. "Nice to meet you too." He smiled.

I sighed, silently happy that Thomas seemed to accept Roar as easily as he accepted everyone else.

"Since when do you have a boyfriend?" Thomas turned to me. "I haven't heard anything about this."

I blushed a little. "It hasn't been that long. We're pretty new."

That was putting it mildly, but if Thomas knew we'd only been together for a few days... well, I didn't think he'd judge me, but it would still be weird.

Roar and I had come so long in such a short period of time. Not everyone would understand that. We just clicked. Sometimes it happened, and it was weird and it was wonderful and it was so *right*.

"I'm about to make dinner," Thomas said. "Do you two you want any?"

"What are you planning on making?"

"I haven't actually had the time to look in the fridge yet, but I think we've got some minced beef, so I figured maybe spaghetti."

"Is anyone else home to eat?"

Thomas shook its head. "Alex and Leo left

yesterday and Ben hasn't been home since Saturday, so it's just the three of us."

So that meant Roar would only have to meet my uncle for now. That was okay. I didn't want to overwhelm him with my family, after all. They could be a little overwhelming sometimes, especially Ben.

I nodded my confirmation that we would join for dinner.

"I'll call when it's done."

So Roar and I headed upstairs.

"Your uncle is really chill," Roar said as he deposited his rucksack next to my desk. He fell onto my bed, stretching out so much his shirt rode up to expose his stomach—and his dark-blond treasure trail.

"He is." I put my own rucksack down next to Roar's, then went over to the bed.

He stared up at me as I loomed over him, then I climbed onto the bed and straddled his thighs. He lay pliant under me and I leaned over to grab onto his wrists, lips hovering over his.

"I know it hasn't been long, that we've skipped a few turns, but..." I stared into his eyes. "I might be a little bit in love with you."

He blinked once, tongue peeking out to lick his lips.

My stomach clenched as the silence stretched—

afraid he didn't feel the same. I'd been so sure he did, but maybe I'd been wrong.

He drew in a sharp breath, gaze flicking from one of my eyes to the other.

"Me too," he finally said, and my stomach instantly unclenched. "But I'm not any good at this."

"This?" I asked, confused.

"Intimacy. Relationships. I've never had good role models, after all."

I chuckled darkly. "Just do the opposite of what your role models did, and I think you'll be fine."

"And if I'm not?" His gaze still flickered between mine.

"Then we'll work on it." I wasn't ready to let him go. Whatever lay ahead, we'd figure it out. I didn't think we'd always get along, that we wouldn't hit rough patches, because we would. Everyone did.

But I cared about him—and we had something real, and it would be worth working through. And if it didn't work, well, then at least I'd tried. We'd tried.

That was all we could do, right?

When he didn't say anything else, I kissed him. Better put those lips to use, after all.

"How about a quickie before dinner?" I asked, grinding down against him. I could feel he wanted it —but he didn't press for anything else but the kiss.

"Spaghetti doesn't take that long to make."

"The whole point of a quickie is that it's *quick*," I pointed out drily.

He chuckled. "I just met your uncle. I don't want him to catch us banging—or smell like we've just been doing it when we go down to eat."

I rolled my eyes and rolled over to lie against his side. "Why are you so *proper*? You're supposed to be the bad boy. Dangerous."

"I'm not bad nor am I dangerous. Unless people deserve it, anyway."

I tilted my head to the side so I could look at his profile. "People are afraid of you."

"Because they don't know me."

"Because you don't let anyone close. Because you always show up with cuts and bruises on your face." I knew he wasn't dangerous—I knew it was his step-father who mostly was the cause of it all. But he wasn't always, because Roar never shied away from a fight. Not one that deserved his attention anyway.

"Cuts and bruises on my face... yeah." He sighed. "It's weird, that. When it's me, who's branded as a troublemaker, they figure I've just been out there making trouble, you know, without asking questions. But if *you'd* shown up at school all the time like that, they would've done something instantly."

I chewed my bottom lip. "No one ever did anything for you?"

He shook his head.

I sighed. "It's not fair."

"But it's the way it is." He didn't seem too bothered by it, but then he did have an excellent poker face.

"Everything'll be different from now on." I grabbed his hand and twined our fingers together. "We've only got a few months left of upper secondary, then it's off to greater things."

"If only I knew what I wanted to do." He sounded defeated.

I sat up, let go of his hand, and headed over to my desk to grab my laptop. Then I settled back on my bed, sitting up against the wall, and patted the space next to me. "Come up here."

"What are you doing?" He propped up on his elbows, gaze curious.

"We're going to take some tests. Career tests. See if that can help you narrow it down."

He scooted backwards, pushed himself up into a sitting position, and settled next to me. "You think a career test is going to help?"

"It sure can't hurt. Maybe it'll help narrow things down for you. You can figure out what you're good at, and maybe some of the suggested jobs stand out." I clicked into my web browser and started Googling. "That way you can apply for school. You could just do a year course if you're not sure and then either apply to get into the bachelor program or do something else. Lots of people take year courses because they don't know what they want."

Google came up with lots of results and I clicked into the first link.

"What are your grades like?" I asked, casting him a look.

"They're okay." He shrugged.

"If your results come back for lawyer or whatever else fancy you'd need a really good average for, would you get in?" I teased.

He didn't look at me, just stared at the screen. "I would, yeah."

"Yeah?" I hadn't expected that, so to say I was surprised...

He sighed, glanced at me, then rubbed awkwardly at his neck. "I've got top grades in all my classes."

I blinked, shocked now. Now *that* I'd never expected. "You got sixes in *everything*?"

"Yeah." More awkward scratching at his neck. "There was this one time I got a five, but I didn't get to study beforehand because my step-dad... well. You know."

So he did better in school than me, and I figured I did pretty well. My average was just under five, though. Or it had been last year anyway, because back when I'd been dating Magnus I'd let my schoolwork go a little. I did better this year, so I hoped by the end of the semester—and with the final exams—I'd jump above the five.

"So you're smart?"

"I study a lot. It's not like I've ever had anything better to do." He reached over and placket the laptop from my lap. "Now let's get on with this."

I could tell he was embarrassed, so I let the subject drop.

"Okay, let's do this." He clicked on the button to start the test.

I leant against his shoulder, reading the questions along with him for a little while until I zoned out. He was fully focus on the screen, and I sat back to take in his profile. The slight stubble on his jaw, the way he bit down on his bottom lip when he wasn't sure what to answer on a question, and the way his lips pressed into a thin line when he was determined.

I never would've thought, that night I met Roar in the park, that we'd end up like this.

In a relationship, a couple, planning our future careers in my bedroom.

I couldn't say I loved him yet—it was way too early for such deep-rooted feelings. But that I *was* falling in love with him, that was for sure. He wasn't at all like everyone else thought he was, he wasn't the bad boy he'd been portrayed as.

I hoped he'd figure out what to do once school was over—and that it would be in or around Trondheim so we could be close when autumn rolled around. Maybe even live together. That would be nice.

And all domestic.

I'd never pictured living with a boyfriend before —certainly never Magnus, who'd been a pig when it came to *everything*.

But Roar?

Yeah, I could picture living with him.

And I had hopes that we'd last so long that we *would* be able to live together.

We were in a good place. Great even—if only he didn't have to deal with that arsehole stepfather of his anymore.

Maybe I'd speak to Thomas about it—maybe he'd let Roar move in officially, like Alex did last year.

It worked out great for Andreas—he got to have Alex around all the time, and they were still together. Even with Andreas gone for a year in the army, they were going strong.

I wanted Roar to be a part of our family the way Alex had become.

I wanted him around, safe and sound, without

the fear of his stepfather every time he went home. I wanted *this* to be his home.

"What are you thinking so hard about?"

I startled at his voice. "Nothing special. Well, that I like having you around. That you should *stay* around."

He turned his head towards me—and I tilted mine up so our lips brushed softly.

"I like being around too," he murmured.

"Good." That was *very* good. Because as long as we were in this good place we were in right now, I wasn't about to let him go.

I wasn't codependent on him, far from, I could be separated from him. But I also didn't want him hurt, so I wasn't about to let him head back to his stepfather unless it was really important. Roar deserved to live a place where he wasn't afraid of a beating, somewhere where people loved and cared about him.

I did.

Cared about him anyway—and was partly on my way to the love part.

"How about you finish that test later?" I asked, voice going husky.

He grinned. "What if I want to finish it right now?"

I put my hand over his lap, quite boldly, and felt

him up. "Are you going to ignore this for a *test*?" He was half-hard.

"Maybe." But his breath caught as I cupped him. "Or maybe not." He leant over to gently put the laptop on the floor, then he rolled over to pin me to the bed. "You're such a distraction. I thought you wanted me to take that test."

"I do." I just wanted to feel him close more right now. This newfound, giddy feeling wouldn't last forever—better enjoy it while it lasted.

And he had a month to apply for schools. All the time in the world, whereas we didn't have much before dinner.

Speaking of dinner…

Thomas called from downstairs—and I groaned and thudded my head back, hitting the headboard.

He laughed, but cupped the back of my head tenderly. "You okay?"

"Just frustrated."

"You knew there'd be dinner." He pushed up and away from me, scrambling onto the floor. Then he held a hand out to me, who still lay in the same position he'd left me in. "Come on, let's go eat. Get to know your uncle a little."

"All right then." I grabbed his hand, let him pull me to my feet. It was almost like the night we met, except then I'd been shivering on a bench and he'd offered to take me home.

He stared down at me, brown eyes dark and fathomless.

"I never imagined, that night, that we'd end up like this," I told him truthfully, not letting go of his hand.

"Me neither." His gaze searched my face for something I couldn't tell.

"Yet here we are."

He stepped closer, crowding into my personal bubble. "Yeah."

I loved his eyes, I could get lost in them, drown in them. They held so much emotion right now, emotion he usually kept hidden away. But it was all open, all there for me to see. Because he *trusted* me.

I kissed him—I couldn't help it. But I couldn't let it turn into anything more, because dinner was ready and Thomas waited downstairs for us.

"Come on, let's go down and have a proper, home cooked meal with family." I opened the door and led him out into the hall. "You don't have to be nervous. Thomas is great."

"I want him to like me," he admitted in a low voice as we moved towards the stairs. "I don't want him to think I'm not good enough for you."

"He won't think that," I assured him, absolutely

certain of it. "Thomas likes everyone. He's good like that."

Roar gave me a small smile—but my words didn't seem to lessen his nervousness any. It didn't matter anyway—he'd soon figure out how great my family was.

"You're great, Roar. They'll all love you."

He snorted, not at all certain of that, but I was. I knew my family. I knew Thomas would take Roar in if it came to that. I knew no one would judge him or not like him, because there wasn't anything unlikeable about him. He was great—when he let his guard down, and kept his temper in check.

In not too long, he'd fit right in, I was sure of it.

ABOUT THE AUTHOR

TT lives in Norway and writes about gay men living in Norway. She also occasionally writes about gay men living in the UK, because she loves the UK. Norway might be too cold for her, but TT doesn't like the summer, so she's learned to adapt. TT is happiest in front of her computer, creating emotional stories about men loving other men.

www.ttkove.com
ttkove@gmail.com